"I am not on the market for some brief, meaningless relationship."

Caleb returned her gaze. "Cat," he murmured softly. "First, no matter what opinion you may have formed of me, I am not in the market for some brief, meaningless relationship, either! Secondly, I have a three-year-old son asleep upstairs, so if you think I can be seduced into bed later, forget it!"

Her mouth opened. And then closed. And then opened again. "I wasn't going to ask!" Cat finally found her voice.

Caleb grinned at her outraged expression. "Seduction isn't asking, Cat, it's exactly what it sounds like—gentle persuasion!"

"Gentle persuasion" with this man would be like using a cap gun against a tank! "I'm not into 'persuasion,' either," she told him sharply. "Gentle or otherwise!"

CAROLE MORTIMER says: "I was born in England, the youngest of three children—I have two older brothers. I started writing in 1978, and have now written one hundred books for Harlequin®.

"I have four sons, Matthew, Joshua, Timothy and Peter, and a bearded collie dog called Merlyn. I'm married to Peter senior. We're best friends as well as lovers, which is probably the best recipe for a successful relationship. We live on the Isle of Man."

Books by Carole Mortimer

HARLEQUIN PRESENTS®
2039—TO WOO A WIFE*
2043—TO BE A HUSBAND*
2051—TO BE A BRIDEGROOM*
*Bachelor Brothers

CAROLE MORTIMER

A Man to Marry

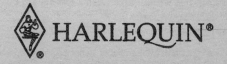

HARLEQUIN®

TORONTO • NEW YORK • LONDON
AMSTERDAM • PARIS • SYDNEY • HAMBURG
STOCKHOLM • ATHENS • TOKYO • MILAN • MADRID
PRAGUE • WARSAW • BUDAPEST • AUCKLAND

For Peter

ISBN 0-373-12086-9

A MAN TO MARRY

First North American Publication 2000.

Copyright © 1999 by Carole Mortimer.

Visit us at www.romance.net

PROLOGUE

'FOR goodness' sake, Gemma, get out of bed, get dressed, and leave! She'll be here any minute!'

'She' had already arrived...

Cat had stopped outside the door of the apartment, and knocked, only for that door to open slightly because it hadn't been closed properly. Very remiss of Graham, Cat had thought as she'd quietly entered. But now she knew it wasn't absent-mindedness that had caused the omission; it had been another impulse completely!

Cat didn't move, couldn't move, held motionless by the sound of Graham—the man she had believed loved her and wanted to marry her—asking some female—Gemma—to get out of his bed...!

'I hope this creeping about won't go on much longer, Graham,' the woman, Gemma, told him in a bored voice. 'Why don't you just ask her what you want to know? And while you're at it—' there was a rustle of movement in the bedroom as Gemma obviously got out of bed '—ask her for *my* engagement ring back; the girls in the office are starting to ask questions about why I'm not wearing it any more!'

Cat looked down at the ring on her left hand, a diamond solitaire that Graham had given her when he'd asked her to marry him a week ago! A diamond solitaire, it transpired, that really belonged to—Gemma!

'It won't be for much longer, Gem,' Graham assured his companion soothingly. 'We're supposed to be discussing wedding plans this evening—'

'That's something I would like to discuss too—*our* wedding plans,' Gemma told him sharply.

'As soon as I have this story in the bag,' Graham promised eagerly. 'I'll be able to get thousands of pounds for it. I may even consider taking it abroad; the appeal is going to be international, after all!'

Story? What story? But did Cat really need to ask? There was only one story in her life that was worth all the trouble Graham had taken to get close to her: first a whirlwind courtship, then an engagement—albeit forged with Gemma's ring!

Tears blurred Cat's vision now. She had believed Graham when he told her he was a wealthy businessman, that he travelled a lot, which was why they couldn't meet as often as she would have liked. She had believed him too when he'd told her he had fallen in love with her, that he wanted to marry her, that he wanted to settle down with her. They had even discussed having children together!

But now it turned out he was nothing but a liar and a cheat, just another reporter trying to get a story, one that would make him rich and famous—and ultimately destroy the life of the person he wanted to write that story about!

'I still don't see—'

'You keep missing the point, Gemma, that's why.' Graham sounded impatient. 'Wedding plans means meeting her family and friends. And once that happens I have my story!'

That was what *he* thought! Cat might have been duped, but now that she knew what Graham really wanted *he* was the one in for a nasty surprise. She slipped the diamond ring off her finger and placed it conspicuously on the coffee-table, so that he would realise exactly what had happened. And the reason why he wasn't going to get his story, or make his fortune.

She left the apartment as quietly as she had entered it.
She didn't look back.
She knew she never would.
But she would never trust a man again, either...

CHAPTER ONE

'REALLY, Toby, do try a more original approach!' Cat laughed up at him as she lay full-length on the swinging garden seat. Her jean-clad legs were stretched comfortably over Toby's thighs as he sat at the other end of the seat. 'Offering to sleep with me to stop speculation in the village that Kate and I are having a "relationship"!' she added derisively, green eyes still laughing at him. 'You've been reading too many cheap and nasty newspapers!'

He shook his head, handsome in a roguish, unkempt sort of way, hair overlong, jeans faded, his shirt frayed at the collar and cuffs. But his casual appearance belied the true state of his finances, Cat was sure. Toby was a highly successful artist; he just liked to look the part of struggling in a garret!

'It just isn't natural for two beautiful, unattached women to live with the grandmother of one of them in this big old house,' Toby protested. 'And with not a man in sight between the three of you!'

'*You're* in sight,' Cat replied mockingly. 'At least, you seem to be here sharing a lot of meals with us!' The four of them had finished eating Sunday lunch together half an hour ago; Kate's grandmother had gone for a lie-down, Kate was still in the house somewhere, and Cat and Toby had opted for sitting in the garden. 'I wouldn't worry about Kate and me too much, if I were you,' Cat continued derisively as he looked about to protest once again. 'The village probably think the three of *us* are involved in a *ménage à trois*!' she dismissed airily, not taking his earlier suggestion in the least seriously.

Toby suggested going to bed with either Kate or herself at least once a week, and had done so since they'd all become friends several months ago. In fact, it would probably be disappointing if he stopped now! But, by the same token, he would probably run a mile if either of them took him up on his offer. However, he was amusing company, fun to have around, and so Cat and Kate didn't mind too much playing along with the game.

His gaze sharpened with interest at her comment. 'Do you really think they do?' He obviously liked the idea.

Cat laughed once more at his boyishly pleased expression. 'I'm sure of it,' she confirmed teasingly, feeling as if she were the elder, although at thirty-five Toby was ten years her senior. To her he was like a mischievous younger brother—and just as harmless. 'Now if—'

'Cat? Cat, for goodness' sake, where are you?' Kate could be heard calling as she left the house to come into the high-walled garden to look for them.

Toby had hunkered down in the garden seat at the first sound of Kate's voice, grimacing across at Cat. 'The dragon lady cometh,' he muttered conspiratorially. 'Let's keep quiet, and maybe she'll go away,' he added hopefully.

His hope would be in vain; they both knew that. When Kate had that determined note in her voice, nothing stopped her!

'That was unkind.' Cat smacked Toby playfully on the arm as she moved her weight up onto her elbows, the movement setting the seat swinging as she looked over the top of the floral back cushions.

Kate stood on the paved patio, a frown marring her brow as she looked for Cat and Toby, but it was a facial expression that did nothing to detract from the beautiful perfection of her face, her hair shining golden in the warm summer sunlight, her body tall and shapely in the businesslike skirt and blouse she had changed into since lunch.

'Over here, Kate,' Cat called to her friend, giving her a friendly wave.

'What on earth did you do that for?' Toby mumbled accusingly at her side.

Cat gave him an affectionate grin. 'We'll take, "Don't you want children of your own rather than looking after other people's all day?" as read, Toby,' she responded drily. 'And my usual refusal to let you father my baby!'

He scowled at her levity. 'Why is it that neither of you take me seriously?' he grumbled. 'The village girls seem to think I'm bohemian and interesting, whereas you and Kate treat me like a naughty little boy who has to be kept in my place!'

There was no doubting Toby's rakish good looks, or the fact that, despite his untidy appearance, he was a very wealthy man, his last three exhibitions in a prestigious London gallery, complete sell-outs. But it was also a sad fact of life, despite his arrival several times a week for a meal, and the occasional evenings he took the two younger women out for the evening, that neither of them took him seriously.

Cat swung her legs to the floor, sitting up on the seat as she heard Kate walking over to where they sat beneath the apple tree. 'Being only children ourselves, it's quite nice to have a naughty "younger" brother,' she assured Toby lightly before turning to smile at Kate as she stood in front of them. 'Everything okay?' she prompted lightly.

'Fine,' Kate nodded. 'You two look comfortable,' she sighed as she dropped down onto the middle cushion of the padded seat. 'It's a shame to disturb you, Cat.' She grimaced. 'But we have a father arriving in half an hour,' she reminded her.

Cat had completely forgotten! 'Time to go and change into my other life.' She stood up, stretching like the feline after which she was called, her curling hair a deep, vibrant red, green eyes twinkling brightly in an impishly attractive face, skin tanned a deep honey-brown from the amount of time she had spent in the warm summer sunshine.

'You have one of the parents coming here on a Sunday?' Toby sounded disgusted at the idea. 'Don't they realise you need some time to yourselves?'

'A parent is a parent all the time, Toby,' Kate rebuked him.

As joint proprietors of the only playschool in the area, Kate and Cat were permanently on call for the parents of the children put in their care through the week.

'Besides,' Kate went on, 'this is a prospective new parent, so we have to make a good impression if we want to stay in business. And being unavailable simply because it's a Sunday isn't going to do that!'

'It's the reason we live in this "big old house", Toby,' Cat told him wryly. 'We needed somewhere big enough for us all to live as well as provide space for the facilities we wanted to open the playschool.'

The years since they'd opened had been successful, much more so than they could ever have hoped for. Although, as Kate had pointed out, they were answerable to the parents of the pre-school children they cared for, and a new parent was someone they wouldn't turn away, despite the inconvenience of a Sunday appointment. Besides, it was because the parents were working in the week that they needed their children to come to a playschool in the first place!

Anyway, Caleb Reynolds had been most insistent that a Sunday afternoon appointment was suitable for him…!

'Pour Kate some lemonade while I go and change,' she told Toby briskly. 'I'll be with you in ten minutes, Kate,' she promised, hurrying towards the house as Toby moved obediently to pour the lemonade.

Cat shook her head ruefully. Good-looking, successful, charming, more than available—and yet there was something missing from Toby's make-up as far as she was concerned. Excitement. That was it! Toby wasn't in the least exciting, had no edge of danger, emitted no challenge to an interested female.

Whereas the man who arrived promptly at three o'clock for his appointment definitely exuded all of those things!

In fact, Cat decided as she looked across the room at him, Kate having opened the door to him and brought him through to their private sitting-room, where they had decided to carry out the interview, he probably exuded too much of them!

Over six feet tall, with dark hair cut short and sprinkled with grey at the temples, cool grey eyes in a sharply hewn face, those cold grey eyes looking down the length of his arrogant nose as he returned her gaze unblinkingly.

Although probably only three or four years Toby's senior, this man had an air of sophistication, of experience, that Toby, for all his bohemian affectations, could never hope to acquire!

Caleb Reynolds' shoulders were wide and powerful, his waist tapered in the charcoal-grey suit he wore, his white shirt pristine, his unpatterned blue tie looking as if it was made of silk. Yes, he looked strong and deeply masculine, and yet it was power of another kind that he radiated as he looked at them both so confidently.

Cat was so stunned by Caleb Reynolds' effect on her that for a few moments she completely overlooked the little boy peeping out at her from behind his legs. Parents were often undecided about bringing their children along with them for this initial meeting, preferring to view the play-school themselves before introducing it to their kids. Caleb Reynolds had obviously felt no such qualms where his son was concerned. But then, he wasn't a three-and-a-half-year-old being confronted by the unknown! As Cat looked at the little boy she could see, by the way he hung back, just how apprehensive he was, brown eyes huge in the paleness of his face.

Cat's heart immediately went out to him. She loved children, and with his shy, obviously nervous manner Caleb Reynolds' son looked more in need of that love than the majority of young children who came here. Most of the girls and boys they cared for on a day-to-day basis were usually more in need of recreation and stimulation while their parents were at work than they were of actual love. But Caleb Reynolds, with his expensive tailored suit and silk tie, and those handmade black shoes, didn't look anything like those parents!

'My associate, Caitlin Rourke,' Kate introduced, making Cat aware that her assessment of Caleb Reynolds and his small son could only have lasted a few moments at the most. 'Cat, this is Mr Reynolds, and this is…?' She gave the little boy an encouraging smile.

'Adam,' his father put in abruptly, reaching down to gently prise the little boy's fingers from the leg of his trousers before gently pulling him round to stand in front of him, his hands resting lightly but firmly on the child's narrow shoulders. 'Adam Reynolds. My son,' the man added, slightly defensively, Cat thought, almost as if he expected someone to challenge him on this last statement.

Cat felt sure not too many people challenged this particular man about anything! Although it was easy, looking at father and son, to see why he felt defensive: the two were nothing alike, as she'd already noted. Caleb was tall and dark, with those arctic grey eyes, but his son was small—small for his age!—with honey-blond hair and huge dark brown eyes.

'I'm very pleased to meet you, Adam.' Cat moved forward, going down on her haunches to shake the little boy's hand, her own gaze warm as she looked into those shy brown eyes. Adam's hand, as it slowly shook hers, was tiny and light to the touch, almost like the wings of a little bird. Cat frowned her inner concern; Adam Reynolds seemed very delicate for a boy of three and a half...

'Adam hasn't been well.' His father spoke sharply when Cat looked at him frowningly as she straightened. 'But he's better now,' he amended harshly.

Cat continued to look at Caleb Reynolds. It wasn't unusual for a father to want to view the playschool his child would attend, but it was usually in accompaniment with his wife. Where was Adam's mother, Caleb Reynolds' wife?

'I'll go and get us all some tea,' Kate offered efficiently. 'Would you like to come with me and get some juice, Adam?' she asked gently, the impatience she felt with the majority of adults never in evidence when she spoke to or was with children.

If anything Kate loved children even more than Cat did, and they instinctively loved her in return, seeming to sense the kindness that dwelt beneath her slightly austere manner. So it came as no surprise to Cat when Adam walked shyly across the room to accompany Kate out to the kitchen, the little boy pausing only once, as he reached the door, the reassuring nod he received from his father enough for him to continue on his way with Kate.

'Amazing!' Caleb Reynolds breathed softly, staring at the doorway through which his son had just left the room. 'Adam has refused to leave my side, even for a minute, for the last six months,' he rasped by way of explanation of his surprise as Cat looked at him questioningly.

'What happened six months ago?' she prompted huskily.

'His mother died,' Caleb Reynolds told her bluntly, his gaze once again seeming to challenge Cat.

It was a starkly made statement, and all the more telling because of the way it was phrased. He hadn't said his wife had died, but that Adam's mother had. Although, as

Adam's father, the child's mother must have meant something to him too...?

'They were involved in a car accident,' Caleb Reynolds continued economically. 'Alicia was killed, Adam was thrown out of the car on impact and broke his arm. I wasn't with them at the time.' The words were bitten out, as if he expected some sort of criticism for his explanation.

It wasn't Cat's place to question or criticise what he chose to tell her. Besides, she had a feeling this man had punished himself enough for the last six months!

'Adam is a beautiful child,' she returned diplomatically.

What else could she say? She didn't know this man. Or his son. Or Adam's mother. She merely needed to know something of Adam's background if he were to come to the playschool, and realised that Caleb Reynolds was aware of that too; she had the feeling that under normal circumstances he would have to be placed on the rack to divulge much of his family history! But, to his credit, it was evidence of how much he loved Adam that he was telling her those things now...

Caleb Reynolds looked troubled, his expression coldly forbidding. 'Adam hasn't spoken for six months.' The words seemed forced out of him.

Cat gave a pained frown, thinking of that beautiful child, a prisoner in a world of silence. 'Since the accident,' she confirmed softly.

'Shock,' Caleb Reynolds explained tersely. 'Do you mind if we sit down?' he asked. 'At the moment I feel like a little boy myself, brought to the headmaster's study for a reprimand for some misdemeanour!'

She very much doubted his feelings particularly bothered him; he was far too self-assured and arrogant for that. But maybe he wouldn't seem so damned patronising if he were sitting in an armchair instead of towering over her!

'Please—take a seat,' she invited curtly. 'You were telling me about Adam,' she reminded him once they were both seated, Caleb in one of the armchairs, Cat on the sofa that faced him.

Caleb sighed heavily. 'He hasn't spoken since they found him after the accident. He understands what is being said to him, responds to anything asked of him—sometimes too readily! He just never—' Caleb broke off, shaking his head, breathing deeply in his agitation.

'What was Adam like before the accident?' Cat enquired softly, wondering if Adam would be able to come here. If he didn't readily leave his father... She certainly couldn't see Caleb Reynolds spending his days with fifteen mischievous children!

The harshly hewn face opposite hers relaxed into a brief smile, giving Cat a glimpse of a man who was relaxed and humorous. If anything he was even more devastatingly attractive like that!

'Until six months ago Adam was like any other mischievous three-year-old,' Caleb Reynolds revealed huskily. 'He laughed all the time.' He was no longer looking at Cat, his thoughts all inwards as he remembered. 'He knew no danger. Accepted no limits. But it's his laughter I miss the most,' he admitted gruffly. 'To come home and hear the sound of his laughter after a frustrating day at work...' He shook his head. 'Adam was a warm and loving child, full of fun,' he finished abruptly, once again looking at Cat, his eyes bleak now.

Cat swallowed hard. This man had not only lost his wife six months ago, but the son he had known and loved had been replaced with a little boy who seemed nervous of his own shadow. He—

'Here we are,' Kate announced brightly as she came in with a laden tea-tray. 'I hope you don't mind, Mr Reynolds, but I took Adam on a tour of the playschool while the kettle was boiling. He was most impressed with the slides and

swings we have outside in the garden, weren't you, Adam?'
she said as she handed him his juice and placed a cake on
a plate on the table in front of him where he now sat on
the sofa beside Cat.

The little boy grinned and nodded his head before picking up the chocolate cake and biting into it hungrily.

'Nothing wrong with your appetite,' Kate murmured
with satisfaction before turning to the two other adults in
the room. 'Tea?' she prompted Caleb Reynolds.

'No sugar, thank you,' he nodded, watching his son with
anxious eyes.

As Cat watched the two of them over the rim of her own
teacup she realised how much love was contained in Caleb
Reynolds for his son. For all that the man looked austere
and unapproachable, slightly disdainful when he looked
down that arrogant nose of his, Caleb Reynolds loved his
son very much. So he had one redeeming feature, after all!

'This is a wonderful old house,' Caleb remarked casually, drinking his tea but ignoring the plate of cake and
biscuits Kate had brought in to accompany it.

'Thank you,' Kate accepted warmly, Cat leaving her
friend to take charge of the conversation now; the last ten
minutes alone with Caleb Reynolds hadn't exactly been
relaxing! 'We're both very fond of it,' Kate continued
pleasantly. 'And, of course, it's ideal for our purposes,' she
stated practically.

Caleb Reynolds nodded. 'And is there a Mr Rourke and
a Mr Brady?'

'No.' Cat was the one to answer him drily, looking
across at him with mocking green eyes, wondering if he
was yet another person who had come to the completely
wrong conclusion concerning the relationship between herself and Kate!

He gave her a narrow-eyed look, but added nothing to
his earlier remark. Not because he didn't want to, Cat felt

sure, but because he could see the defiance in her expression, and was determined not to give her the satisfaction of meeting it!

'I'm renting a cottage in the village,' he bit out abruptly. 'Rose Cottage. I don't know if you know it?'

'We do,' Kate answered with a smile; considering how small the village was, they would be particularly insular if they didn't! 'You don't intend staying in the area long, then, Mr Reynolds?'

'That all depends,' he said noncommittally.

'Don't look so worried, Mr Reynolds.' Cat laughed softly at his suddenly cagey expression. 'The length of your stay won't affect whether or not Adam is accepted here.'

He returned her gaze with those cool grey eyes for several long seconds before replying. 'I wasn't worried,' he finally drawled.

She doubted very much ever worried this man, certainly not being accepted. For one thing, she was sure his obvious wealth usually assured him a smooth—and comfortable!—passage wherever he chose to go. And, for another, it didn't look as if it would bother him too much if it didn't!

'Do you have work in the area?' Kate asked politely, much more the capable of the two of them when it came to dealing with the parents, which was why Cat usually left the lead to her in interviews like this.

'Not exactly.' Once again his answer was designed to tell them as little about himself as possible.

As Cat had guessed all too easily a short time ago, Caleb Reynolds was not a man who liked, or wanted, to talk about himself. She was sure he had only told her what he had earlier because in the circumstances he'd felt he had to.

But he obviously didn't have too much of an idea about village life, because what Lilley Stewart, at the post office and general store, didn't know about any of the local residents usually wasn't worth anything! And, as the newest inhabitant, Caleb Reynolds was sure to be the favourite topic of conversation for several weeks. Whether they were interested or not, anyone who went into the post office for so much as a stamp in the next few weeks would be told what little Lilley already knew about him, and pumped for any information they might have that she didn't!

With Caleb's young son in their care five mornings a week, Kate and Cat would definitely be in the line of fire. Village life certainly had its disadvantages as well as its advantages!

'I'm really of very little interest,' Caleb drawled as he seemed to half guess her thoughts. 'Although I believe you've had your share of public figures living in the village.' He smartly turned the conversation away from himself.

A fact that didn't go unnoticed by Cat. He really didn't want to talk about himself, did he? Although she couldn't say she was exactly happy with the direction the conversation had taken now...

'At least, you did,' Caleb added drily, when neither she nor Kate made any response to his initial comment.

'Oh, you must mean Toby Westward,' Cat dismissed lightly. 'Our colourful—literally!—local artist. He was just here for lunch, actually.' She was starting to be defensive now, had been feeling that way since Caleb Reynolds had asked if either of them was married. What was wrong with society today if two women couldn't live and work together without creating gossip and speculation?

'Was he?' Caleb Reynolds acknowledged without interest. 'Actually, I was referring to Katherine Maitland. In fact, I believe she actually lived in this house at one time.'

If he had tossed a bomb amongst them he couldn't have sent stronger shock waves through the room, both Kate and Cat staring at him with wide, disbelieving eyes.

'Where on earth did you hear that?' Kate was finally the

one to gasp, Cat still staring at Caleb as the prey must stare at the snake—just before it strikes the fatal blow.

He shrugged. 'The woman at the post office mentioned it to me yesterday when I went in to pick up supplies,' he responded, his mouth twisting into a wry smile. 'A bit of local colour! I believe she did mention Toby Westward, too,' he finished.

Obviously Toby held no interest for him whatsoever! But Katherine Maitland did...

'No doubt you're on her list of 'local colour' too now,' Cat put in hardly. 'And I believe you may be right about Katherine Maitland once having owned this house; I seem to recall it being mentioned when we first looked at the place with a view to buying.' She deliberately didn't look at Kate as she spoke.

'Although she can't have lived here for years. Way before our time.' She silently congratulated herself on having dealt with the situation so calmly.

'Very much so,' Caleb Reynolds accepted. 'Although you will obviously have heard of her?' He raised dark brows.

'Of course.' Kate was the one to take over their side of the conversation this time. 'She was one of the most famous opera singers of her day. But surely she must be dead by now?' she queried flippantly. 'She must be ancient!'

His mouth twisted again. 'Early seventies at a guess,' he said. 'Hardly ancient. I actually saw her perform once, shortly before she retired,' he continued huskily. 'It's something I've never forgotten. She didn't only have the most amazing voice, she had something else, a charisma that was electric!'

'But—' Cat broke off, breathing deeply. 'You must have been very young?' She kept her voice light.

'Not so young,' he returned. 'Although it must be about

twenty-five years since she retired after a family tragedy. You—'

'Oh, look,' Kate cut in softly. 'We've bored poor Adam into falling asleep!' she said warmly, standing up to cross the room to where the little boy lay back against the cushion behind him, his lashes long and thick as they rested against his cheeks in repose, Kate reaching out to gently smooth the silky hair from his brow.

'He still takes the occasional nap in the afternoon,' his father excused, abruptly standing up. 'I'm quite happy for Adam to start here in the morning, if you are,' he stated arrogantly. 'Unless the two of you would like time to discuss it first?' he questioned, that defensive wall back in place.

Cat glanced across at Kate, knowing they didn't need to talk about it. The father could be a problem, but she knew they both thought Adam was adorable! 'If you think Adam will stay with us?' She looked at him enquiringly.

'He seems quite comfortable with you.' He still sounded surprised by this fact. 'Although we won't know whether or not he will stay with you until we try it,' he added harshly.

Cat had a feeling that it would be good for both father and son to have a break from each other for a few hours. Adam would benefit from being with other children, and it couldn't have been easy for his father to be constantly in demand over the last six months.

'As you say,' she nodded. 'We won't know until we try.'

Caleb looked at her from beneath dark brows for several long seconds, but said nothing more before gently lifting Adam and carrying him out to his car.

'Phew!' Cat muttered once they were back inside the house, collapsing back into one of the armchairs.

'Ditto!' Kate dropped down into the chair opposite, absently stroking their cat as it jumped up onto her knee.

'Adam is adorable,' Cat acknowledged, head back, eyes closed. 'But the father!' She shook her head. 'Arrogant. Cold. So—'

'He loves Adam,' Kate pointed out wearily, obviously having felt the strain of their meeting as much as Cat had.

'He's trouble, Kate; I can feel it!' She grimaced. 'But Adam...' She thought back to that tousle-haired little boy, to the trauma he had suffered that had rendered him speechless. They could help him, she felt sure of it, sensed they had already made a breakthrough when Adam had gone off with Kate, something his father had admitted he hadn't done for the last six months. She relayed to Kate what Caleb had told her in Kate's absence earlier. 'I'm willing to overlook the father if we can be of help to Adam,' she pronounced finally.

'We can try,' Kate said slowly. 'Ignoring the father, I mean. I have a feeling not too many people manage to ignore Caleb Reynolds!'

So did Cat.

Which could, ultimately, be a problem for them. For all of them.

Only time would tell.

Cat stood up decisively. 'Let's go and make another pot of tea and take it through to Kitty.' She was determined to dispel the mood of gloom that had fallen over them since meeting Mr Reynolds. After all, they only thought Caleb Reynolds might be more trouble than looking after his son was worth. He might never mention a particular subject again...

And, if he did, they would deal with the problem when— and if—it became necessary...

CHAPTER TWO

'WHO on earth can that be?' Kate sighed impatiently as the doorbell could be heard ringing as they were about to go outside into the garden. 'Not Toby again!'

Cat smiled at her sympathetically. At the end of a long day, the children all safely returned to their parents, their own leisurely evening meal over and the clearing away completed, they liked nothing better than to relax in the privacy of their garden, making the most of the lighter nights, this evening being a particularly warm one.

The walled garden had offered two positive things when they'd first come to view the house: a safe place for the children to come outside and play in the daytime and complete privacy for themselves in the evenings and at weekends. This evening Kate had obviously been looking forward to a couple of hours' relaxation, either with a good book, or just in gentle, meaningless conversation.

'It's all right,' Cat assured her brightly. 'You go ahead and I'll join you in a few minutes. When I've got rid of Toby!' she amended ruefully, as convinced as Kate that he had to be their unexpected visitor.

They both liked Toby, found him amusing company, but just lately he had taken to calling in on them uninvited, and too much of a good thing was just that—too much!

'It's you he's come to see, anyway,' Kate teased. 'I'm far too bossy for him!'

Cat pushed back her tousled red curls, shaking her head. 'Then he obviously hasn't taken note of my fiery Irish temper! I'll be five minutes behind you—max!' she promised determinedly. It had been a long day for her too, and the last thing she felt like doing was fending off Toby's obvious advances—especially as she was sure it was just a game to him.

Kate laughed softly, glowingly lovely, her hair loose about her shoulders. 'I admire your optimism!'

Cat returned her smile before going in answer to the second ringing of the doorbell. The only positive thing about Toby's impromptu visit this evening was that he had arrived after dinner; usually he contrived to arrive right at a mealtime, and expected to be fed!

'The answer is no, Toby, so I'll save you…' Cat's voice trailed off in embarrassed surprise as she opened the door fully and found not Toby standing on the doorstep but Caleb Reynolds!

A completely different Caleb Reynolds from yesterday, she noted, the short-sleeved open-necked blue shirt much more informal than the suit he had worn then, as were the faded denims. Somehow the casualness of his appearance made him seem younger, much less forbidding…

'Mr Reynolds,' she greeted awkwardly, wearing a striped sleeveless tee shirt and faded denims herself. Well, they hadn't been expecting company…

'And not Toby,' he conceded drily, grey gaze lightly mocking. 'Although, as you were saying a very firm no to him, perhaps it's as well!' He quirked dark, mocking brows.

Cat felt the warmth in her cheeks as she looked up at him; at only just five feet in height herself, this man towered over her. 'Sorry about that.' She grimaced. 'Toby is very nice—'

'But?' Caleb Reynolds prompted.

'But' nothing she was about to regale this man with! Toby could be a pest at times, but he was also a friend, and she had no intention of discussing him behind his back with a virtual stranger. 'What can I do for you, Mr Reynolds?' she said briskly; he had seemed more than happy when he'd arrived to pick Adam up at twelve-thirty and found his young son sitting quietly in a corner with Kate doing a jigsaw puzzle. 'There's been no adverse reaction from Adam this evening concerning his morning at playschool, has there?' She frowned concernedly.

'Not so far, no,' he said thankfully. 'Hopefully there won't be one. The thing that bothered me the most about it was getting him to stay in the first place.'

But that had been achieved quite effectively when Kate had taken Adam by the hand and offered to show him again the swings and slides he had been so interested in yesterday...

'I was actually going to telephone you this evening,' Caleb Reynolds continued, looking a little grim. 'But the daughter of the woman I've rented the cottage from offered to babysit Adam this evening, and as he's fast asleep— She seems quite reliable,' he added distractedly. 'And Adam doesn't usually wake up once he's asleep, so I—'

'Jane is very reliable,' Cat assured him, taking pity on him; it must be as difficult for him to leave Adam after what had happened as it was for Adam to leave him! 'She helps out at the playschool part-time during the school holidays. She's taking her A levels.' And now, Cat realised self-disgustedly, *she* was the one babbling.

It was just that Caleb Reynolds was the last person she had expected to see when she'd opened the door. Although she had a feeling Kate would have handled the situation better than she was; tact and diplomacy were not her fortes!

'Would you mind if I came in for a few minutes?' Caleb enquired. 'I won't take up too much of your time,' he said bluntly as Cat looked at him blankly. 'I'm sure, like myself, you have other things to do this evening.'

It wasn't that she didn't want to invite him in, she just wasn't sure it was convenient at the moment. They had all been going out into the garden, and— 'Please, do come in,'

Cat invited stiltedly, thinking fast. 'I—I believe Kate is taking a bath,' she added hurriedly, believing no such thing! 'I'll just go and war—tell her that you're here—'

'That won't be necessary.' He had followed her through into the same room as yesterday. 'Unless you feel in need of the moral support?' he commented derisively, his presence in this utterly feminine room with its chintz curtains and covers once again malely dominating.

Cat bristled indignantly at his mocking tone. Arrogant, patronising—! Her sympathy for him of a few minutes ago completely evaporated. 'Not in the least,' she dismissed scathingly.

Besides, she could imagine Kate right this minute, in the most secluded part of the garden, relaxing on a lounger, Kitty at her side. No, she wasn't about to disturb either of them; she could deal with Caleb Reynolds quite well on her own!

'Please sit down,' she invited tersely, waiting for him to do so but maintaining her own standing position beside the unlit fireplace. 'And if it isn't a problem with Adam that brought you here, then what can we do to help you, Mr Reynolds?' she asked warily. Because this man, with his arrogant disdain, didn't give her the impression he was in the habit of paying social calls just for the sake of it!

He looked at her consideringly for several long seconds, the silence stretching awkwardly between them. 'Miss Rourke—or perhaps I can call you Cat?' he drawled, seeming amused by her continued formality.

And no doubt he was amused, Cat inwardly acknowledged, but she would bet that if she stepped even one inch over what he considered the line to intrusion into *his* private life, rather than the polite interest she had shown so far, he would step on it—and her!—very quickly.

'Please do,' she accepted distantly.

'And I'm Caleb.'

How cosy! And yet she knew that it wasn't. She would take a guess on this man squashing her like a bug if she got in his way! But what way did he want to go...?

'That still doesn't tell me what I can do to help you,' she reminded him. 'If there is no problem with Adam—'

'I've already told you there isn't—Cat,' he returned evenly, that arctic gaze easily capturing and holding hers. 'Adam—for all that I spent the best part of the morning pacing up and down worrying in case he needed me!— seems to have enjoyed his morning here. In fact, I think, if anything, he found the afternoon with just the two of us quite boring. It's always the way with children, isn't it?' He grimaced. 'We get the grey hairs, and they just grow bigger and stronger!'

Cat relaxed slightly at the paternal image of this man pacing up and down in worry over his son. It brought back to her the fact that no matter how arrogant and patronising she found him he did love his son. It was there in his intonation when he spoke of Adam.

'I had never really thought of it in quite that way,' she smiled. 'But yes, I suppose they do. But you really have no need to worry any further about Adam while he's here; the other children didn't seem to mind at all that he didn't actually speak to them. In fact, they seem to have a sort of telepathy with each other at this age!' Considering the trauma Adam had suffered just six months ago, although he had stayed quite close to Cat and Kate during the morning, he had also, to their delight, played with the other children.

'So I've noticed,' Caleb agreed. 'My sister has a little girl of two, and she and Adam have no trouble communicating with each other at all.'

Slowly Cat was learning more about this man, though it was like getting blood from a stone! But she still had a feeling that was more than most people could get out of him. She knew he had been married, that his wife had died, that he had a sister, and a niece. It was probably more than he knew about her, Cat conceded. And that was the way it was going to stay!

Although she couldn't help wondering why, with family obviously living somewhere close—Adam was able to play with his cousin—Caleb Reynolds had chosen to move to this area at all…? Unless his sister lived around here too? But if that was the case why rent a cottage? Why not just stay with his sister? There was still a lot about Caleb Reynolds they *didn't* know!

'I actually came here this evening,' he said softly, 'to ask you and Kate if I could look around your house.'

He had lulled her into a false sense of security by talking about Adam, and then—pow!—he'd hit her with what he was really here for!

Cat stared at him, green eyes wide. 'I thought you were happy with our facilities when I showed you round this morning?' She frowned. 'I can assure you that we are inspected on a regular basis, and—'

'I don't want to look around the playschool again, Cat,' Caleb cut in mildly. 'As you say, I've already seen it, and I have no doubt that it passes inspection. It's actually the rest of the house I'm interested in seeing.'

'Why?' Cat blurted out rudely, too startled for politeness.

'Because it's one of the oldest houses in the area and I have an interest in old houses?' he suggested drily, dark brows raised at her bluntness.

She met his gaze unblinkingly. 'And?'

He shrugged. 'Does there have to be an and?'

She nodded abruptly. 'I think so, yes!'

Why on earth did he want to look around this particular house? Admittedly it was almost one hundred and fifty years old, had originally been the manor house of the area, surrounded by farmland that was worked by the tenants of the cottages in the village. But the squire's family had moved out of the area years ago, the farmland bought up by neighbouring farmers, and the village itself had expanded and grown, so that the nearest dwelling was now only a quarter of a mile away. In fact, it was the cottage this man was currently renting!

Again Caleb gave her that steady, steely-eyed look. But if he thought he was going to unnerve her he was mistaken; as a parent she would treat him with the same politeness she did all their other clients, but as someone wanting to invade the privacy of their home—! The same rules didn't apply in that situation. So Cat met that level gaze with an intensity of her own.

'Okay,' Caleb Reynolds finally murmured, shrugging his shoulders, 'you've guessed my secret.' A charming smile accompanied this statement.

A smile that Cat had no intention of responding to, that put her even more on her guard instead. Charm was not something she particularly associated with this man, so it had to be there now for a reason...

'There is more than just a mild curiosity on my part,' he conceded grudgingly. 'You see—'

'Cat, what on earth is keeping you this long?' Kate called impatiently as she could be heard walking down the hallway. 'Really, Toby, it's been a hard day, and—' Kate was as surprised to see Caleb Reynolds sitting in the room with Cat as Cat had been earlier when she'd opened the door to him. 'Mr Reynolds...?' she greeted in a puzzled voice.

'Miss Brady,' he returned formally, having stood up at her entrance. 'Although your friend and I have decided to dispense with formality and stick to first names,' he added, once again with that charming smile.

If one were in the mood to be charmed—which Cat certainly wasn't! Besides, that smile didn't quite reach the hardness of those icy grey eyes...

'Really?' Kate gave Cat a sideways glance, obviously as confused as Cat had been by his presence here.

Although Cat was no longer as confused as she had been initially. If he thought she had forgotten his 'secret', he was mistaken!

'Did you enjoy your bath, Kate?' he enquired solicitously, his gaze mocking now.

Cat could easily guess the reason for his mockery, on two counts. Firstly, the pieces of grass that were both on the back of Kate's top and entangled in her hair clearly showed she hadn't been anywhere near the bath in the last few minutes. And, secondly, Kate's blankly uncomprehending expression said she didn't have a clue what he was talking about!

Cat had originally used the excuse of Kate being in the bath because she hadn't wanted Caleb to suggest joining them in the garden. But Kate's slightly dishevelled, obviously post-garden appearance simply made a liar out of her.

'My mistake, I'm afraid,' Cat put in sweetly, her expression deliberately bland. 'I thought you had gone to have a bath, but obviously you haven't finished in the garden yet,' she said pointedly.

Kate gave her a frowning look before turning to Caleb. 'Gardens take up such a lot of one's time, don't they?' she said conversationally, her words neither confirming nor belying Cat's statement. 'As you're going to find out while you're at Rose Cottage. Unless you have someone coming in to take care of it for you?'

Cat knew that Jane's mother always did the cleaning at the cottage, and with Adam taken care of as well five mornings a week she couldn't help wondering what Caleb was going to find to do with his time if he passed the gardening on to someone else too. Besides coming here when he felt like it and making a nuisance of himself, that was! One male dropping in unannounced was bad enough; two was intolerable!

'Actually, no,' Caleb answered Kate lightly. 'It was the fact that the cottage had such a large garden that appealed to me. We live in an apartment in London, and the doctors seemed to think that a complete change of scenery might be of benefit to Adam.'

'So *he's* going to do the gardening?' Cat put in, with only a light veil over her sarcasm.

It was a veil that didn't fool Caleb for a moment, and he looked at her consideringly for several seconds. 'You don't like me very much, do you, Cat?' he finally murmured thoughtfully.

Like him—she didn't even know him! But the habit he had of speaking his mind was a little unnerving, yes. Kept between the two of them, it wasn't a problem, but with Kate present—Kate who now looked very uncomfortable with the turn the conversation had taken—it was a completely different matter.

'Kate's the diplomat in this partnership, Caleb,' Cat returned ruefully. 'I have better success dealing with children.'

'As opposed to men?' he returned softly.

'As opposed to anyone!' Cat snapped back, eyes flashing deeply green.

Give me a break, Kate, her expression silently pleaded with her friend; this man gave as good as he got—if not better!

'You were about to explain your interest in seeing around this house?' she prompted their visitor, deliberately not looking at Kate now as she heard her friend's indrawn breath, but hoping that her friend now understood her own defensive attitude towards this man.

Caleb looked perfectly relaxed, seemingly unaware of the underlying tension in the room. 'It's quite simple, really,' he replied. 'I'm interested in this house because my great-great-grandfather was its architect.'

The two women couldn't have felt—or looked!—more stunned if he had told them his ancestor had been Jack the Ripper!

Cat didn't know what explanation she had been expecting, but it certainly hadn't been the one Caleb Reynolds had just given. And poor Kate seemed to be having trouble keeping up with the conversation at all.

'Clive Reynolds,' he explained as their shocked silence continued. 'The house was actually named after him. His name is carved into the stonework on the front of the house,' he added as he still received no response from either of the two women.

Clive Reynolds… He was right, it was. But time and familiarity had dulled for them the awareness of that name and a date, 1850, etched into the stone directly above the front door. Clive Reynolds. This man's great-great-grandfather…

The surname was obviously the same, and yet…

'What a coincidence.' Once again Cat's barely veiled scepticism could be heard, and the sudden hardness of his grey eyes said Caleb Reynolds was well aware of it!

'Not at all,' he bit out crisply. 'I'm in the area because I have some research to do at the museum in York, but I chose this village for my stay deliberately once I realised about the house. I'm curious to know whether or not my ancestor built any other houses in the area.'

'Doubtful,' Cat couldn't resist snapping. 'It's hardly the sort of area that could have supported two such grand houses,' she elaborated as he looked at her icily.

'I'm a historian, Cat,' Caleb Reynolds told her evenly, deliberately seeming to keep all emotion from his voice. Although his eyes were a different matter: hard, glacial, narrowed to icy slits as he looked steadily at Cat. 'But I specialise in architecture. Perhaps only naturally with an architect as an ancestor,' he added almost confrontationally.

Cat didn't see what was 'natural' about it at all; her own father trained and bred horses, but she had always been— to her father's dismay—terrified of them. They were beautiful and powerful to look at and admire from a distance, but completely unpredictable in close proximity, she had found. Exactly like Caleb Reynolds...

She brought her thoughts up short. Really! Caleb Reynolds might be powerful and attractive, but he certainly wasn't beautiful! What on earth was she thinking of? Or maybe she just wasn't thinking at all... And, around this man, that could be dangerous!

He certainly didn't look like any historian she had ever seen, on television or in the newspapers, most of them old and fusty-looking, as if they belonged in the past with their textbooks!

'In the circumstances, I quite understand your interest in this house.' Kate had recovered enough to be able to take over their half of the conversation.

Which was perhaps as well; Cat, with her usual forthright manner, only seemed to be antagonising Caleb Reynolds! His knowledge of at least one past owner of the house was now more easily explained, although why he couldn't have told them all of this yesterday was still a mystery...

'And I'm sure, at some convenient time to all of us, that it could be arranged for you to look round the house,' Kate continued politely. 'Although, as I'm sure you appreciate, the house has been completely modernised over the years!'

'We even have mains sewage nowadays!' Cat put in sharply, ignoring Kate's pained wince. Damn it, the man was the one asking *them* a favour, and a damned inconvenient one at that.

She wished now that it *had* been Toby at the front door

earlier; she wouldn't have had any trouble saying no to any 'secrets' he might have wanted to share!

'I'm sure you do,' Caleb drawled drily, one dark brow raised questioningly at her continued aggression. 'And don't worry, I wasn't asking if I could look round right this minute,' he turned to tell Kate charmingly. 'I more than appreciate the fact that I've rather sprung this on you. I also realise that you have other considerations to take into account.'

Cat looked at him sharply, not fooled for a moment by that charm which he seemed to be able to turn on and off at will—it was usually off when he was talking to her! 'What "other considerations"?' she enquired warily.

'The playschool, of course,' he returned easily. 'I appreciate I couldn't just stroll about during the day when you have all the children in your care.'

She had news for him; he couldn't 'just stroll about' their home when the children weren't here, either! He really was the most—

'There's also Kate's grandmother to consider,' he continued evenly.

Stunned didn't even begin to describe their silence this time—more like electric. This man, completely unknown to them until roughly thirty-six hours ago, knew far too much about their home and them; Cat was absolutely positive that neither she nor Kate had mentioned her grandmother to this man yesterday! But Cat's earlier summing-up of this man still stood; getting information out of *him* that *he* didn't want to give was like getting blood out of a stone. Though he had just spoken readily enough about his reason for being in the area, about his great-great-grandfather being the architect of this house, which was the reason he wanted to look round it, all that information had been volunteered—making Cat wonder exactly what it was he *wasn't* saying!

Cat glanced across at Kate now, seeing all too easily how the colour had faded from her friend's cheeks, the way she looked at Caleb Reynolds in fascinated horror. Once again like the snake and its victim!

'Don't tell me,' Cat put in scornfully. 'Lilley at the post office, again!' She gave a derisive shake of her head. 'Really, Caleb,' she taunted. 'I would never have taken you for the gossiping kind!'

He looked nonplussed. 'I wasn't aware that you had 'taken' me at all, Cat,' he returned mockingly, satisfaction gleaming in his eyes at the way her cheeks suddenly burned. 'But you're right about the gossip,' he continued before she could make any reply to his innuendo. 'When I made my initial enquiries about Clive House I was told that a Miss Brady and a Miss Rourke lived here with Miss Brady's grandmother.'

Innocent enough. It certainly wasn't a secret that Kate's grandmother lived here with them. It was just thoroughly disconcerting that this man should know so much about them! And not just from Lilley at the post office, either... So where had he got his information? And why? So far he had been very cagey about his reason for being in the area. And if he should turn out to be a reporter...! Cat had allowed one reporter too close to her once, no matter how unwittingly, and she wouldn't let it happen again!

He looked at them both with assessing eyes. 'I wasn't aware I was saying something out of turn...?'

'You didn't,' Kate answered him with a return of confidence. 'Kitty—my grandmother—does live here with us. But she isn't in the best of health, has few visitors, and goes out even less, and I would rather talk to her before you look round the house. I think you'll be quite impressed when you see all of it,' she assured him. 'It's really been very well looked after, with a lot of the original features kept in place—'

'He doesn't want to buy the house, Kate,' Cat snapped. 'Just look at it!'

'I can see I've taken up enough of your time for one evening,' Caleb put in sardonically, moving to the door. 'So I'll leave you all in peace.'

Peace? The man didn't know the meaning of the word!

'I'll see you out.' Kate followed him.

'Cat.' He paused at the door to nod abruptly in parting.

'Mr Reynolds,' she returned tersely.

She hadn't moved when Kate returned to the sitting-room a few minutes later, looking up at her friend with bright green eyes. 'He's right,' Cat told Kate fiercely, 'I don't like him!' Her eyes flashed angrily.

'He's—unsettling,' Kate acknowledged more cautiously.

'Kate, the man is arrogant and condescending—and I don't trust him one little bit!'

'Let's not get all of this out of proportion,' Kate warned. 'Admittedly I was a bit surprised when he said he would like to look round the house, but as his great-great-grandfather designed it—'

'So he says!' Cat snapped, scowling darkly. 'Reynolds isn't exactly an uncommon name, Kate,' she pointed out scornfully as her friend looked at her questioningly. 'And he mentioned nothing yesterday about his ancestor having designed this house, only came up with that idea today—when the name is engraved on the front of the house for all to see!'

Kate looked bewildered. 'You don't think Clive Reynolds was his great-great-grandfather...?'

'I think it's all just a little too much of a coincidence,' Cat said firmly. 'But I'm going to find out the truth,' she added determinedly. 'There are bound to be records, some way I can actually find out if he's related to Clive Reynolds. In the meantime, I suggest we say nothing to

Kitty about this. There's no point in bothering her with it until we know for certain.'

'I agree,' Kate said slowly, momentarily closing her eyes. 'Will it ever stop, do you think, Cat?' she added wearily as the two of them strolled back out to the garden.

Cat squeezed her arm reassuringly. 'Of course it will. We've all lived here in relative peace for the last few years; there's no reason why that shouldn't continue.' Caleb Reynolds would be dealt with very firmly if he should turn out to be any other than what he claimed to be. She would see to that. And enjoy doing it, she realised.

'Hello, darlings.' Kitty beamed at them both; Kate's grandmother, who supposedly wasn't in the best of health, at this moment was down on her hands and knees as she weeded a flower bed!

In her early seventies, Kitty nevertheless looked years younger than that, shoulder-length blonde hair swept back from her face, her face relatively unlined by the years, her figure still youthfully slim as she stood up.

Despite the fact that she hadn't performed in public for twenty-five years, she was still, to anyone who had admired and known her—as Caleb Reynolds obviously had!—instantly recognisable as the opera singer, Katherine Maitland!

CHAPTER THREE

'HIS great-great-grandfather *was* Clive Reynolds,' Cat announced crossly as she dropped down into one of the chairs placed around the kitchen table.

She had waited until the playschool closed for the day on Tuesday afternoon before going off in the car to the local library. What she had found there hadn't cheered her up one little bit. She had been so sure there was something about Caleb Reynolds that didn't ring true... But she was unable to refute his claim when it had been printed there in black and white!

'That's wonderful.' Kate sighed her relief at the news. 'You managed to find a book on Clive Reynolds, then?'

'Er—not exactly.' Cat grimaced. 'I found a book on Caleb Reynolds,' she admitted reluctantly. 'Actually, it was a book he's written on the history of English architecture, but it had some blurb about the author inside the cover.' It had been accompanied by a picture of the author, a photograph obviously several years old, no grey visible at the temples in Caleb's dark hair as there was now, a pair of gold-rimmed glasses making him look studious. As photographs went, Cat had decided, it was pretty uninspiring— and nothing of the man's intensity in the flesh came through. 'He apparently became interested in the subject of architecture because of his great-great-grandfather, the architect Clive Reynolds.' She grudgingly made a direct quote from the personal information given about the author of the book.

Kate grinned her relief, that smile starting to slip as she saw Cat was still scowling. 'But that's good news, isn't it?'

'I still don't trust him.' Cat shook her head stubbornly.

'You don't *like* him,' Kate corrected. 'Don't confuse dislike with distrust.'

'Why would someone like him move—even temporarily—to a small village like this?' Cat muttered thoughtfully. Because that information about him inside his book had also listed his qualifications and the achievements he had made in his field; the list of letters behind his name was staggering. Caleb wasn't only intelligent, but obviously deeply respected in his chosen field...

'He already explained all that,' her friend protested at her continued belligerence. 'He has some research to do at the museum in York, and he's interested in seeing round this house,' she reminded her. 'Heavens, Cat, I don't remember this reaction from you towards Toby when he moved into one of the cottages in the village almost a year ago!' She gave Cat an impatient look.

It was true. But then, apart from suggesting that one of them went to bed with him every time they saw him, Toby was harmless enough. And that was one accusation, she was sure, that could never be levelled at Caleb Reynolds!

'Talking about Toby—' Kate grimaced '—he called round earlier. I told him to come back later and have dinner with us. Kitty will enjoy that,' she added before Cat could make any comment about Toby being here for a meal yet again.

Kate had used the right argument to silence Cat; Kitty *would* enjoy having Toby here this evening. Kitty found Toby amusing, enjoyed his company very much, and as he had no idea who she was—or had been!—it meant that Cat and Kate could relax when he was around.

It hadn't been an easy decision to make when it came to buying this particular house to open their playschool. Kitty had lived in it many years ago, and some of the locals still remembered that—including Lilley at the post office, although she, like the other villagers, never told 'outsiders' that Kitty, Kate's grandmother, and Katherine Maitland were one and the same person.

But Clive House had been on the market at the time they were looking for premises for their playschool, and Kitty had been delighted at the idea of returning to the house where she had lived during her married life, where she had brought up her children. To give the villagers their due, once the initial interest had worn off, they had rallied round Kitty in a protective way that didn't allow outsiders into the fact that they had a celebrity—albeit a retired one— living amongst them! For twenty-five years Kitty had stayed out of the public eye, deliberately so; the family tragedy that Caleb had referred to yesterday had given her every reason never to open herself up to that sort of interest ever again.

When Kitty had first made her decision never to sing in public again, she had been hounded for months by news-papers anxious to buy her story. Over the years that intense interest had faded, but the media was always conscious that it could as quickly be revived. But Kitty didn't need that; she enjoyed the calm and tranquillity she had been able to find in the village amongst old friends.

So the buying of Clive House had proved a good deci-sion for all of them, the playschool a great success, and, best of all, Kitty was happy.

But Cat couldn't help her nagging feeling that Caleb's presence here was somehow going to change all that...

'Okay.' She stood up decisively, doing her best to shake off those feelings of gloom; Kate was right, she shouldn't confuse dislike with distrust. Besides, she didn't exactly dislike Caleb... 'What can I do to help prepare this eve-ning's culinary delight?' she offered, determined not to even think of Caleb again tonight.

Kate raised blonde brows. 'But it's my turn to get the

meal tonight. And I thought you hated cooking?' she added teasingly as she got vegetables from the rack.

'I do,' Cat acknowledged just as lightly, taking over the peeling of the carrots. 'If it weren't for you and Kitty, I would just live out of tins!'

Kate nodded smilingly. 'As Kitty is fond of saying, pity the poor man you marry!'

It was a standing joke between the three of them that if Cat ever married it would have to be to someone who knew how to cook himself—or else he would starve!

'And break up this happy trio?' Cat grinned without rancour. 'No way!'

The two of them worked together in companionable silence, this time of day when Kitty, if she wasn't helping with the preparation, usually took her rest. But she would be bright and sparkling this evening for dinner, had lost none of her charm, or the 'electricity', as Caleb had called it, that had endeared her to audiences all over the world at the height of her career.

Damn, Cat had just thought of Caleb again! Why did she keep doing that? What—?

'Good evening, ladies—we were just driving past, and Adam insisted we stop to say hello,' Caleb announced apologetically as Cat had dropped the knife noisily into the sink at the first sound of his voice.

Cat was amazed at his familiarity; he and his son had just walked around to the side door and into the kitchen! Although, to give Caleb his due, he did look a little uncomfortable at the obvious intrusion; it was Adam, silently chuckling as he stood at his father's side, who looked pleased with himself.

'I did ring the front doorbell,' Caleb pleaded as their surprised silence continued. 'But it doesn't seem to be working...'

'Toby mentioned something about it earlier.' Kate grimaced in apology, drying her hands on the towel. 'It must be broken again,' she told Cat.

Cat was still staring at Caleb, so tall and dark and dominating, broodingly attractive in a black shirt and black denims. So much for not even thinking of him again this evening—she didn't need to; he was becoming as regular a visitor as Toby. Albeit this time at Adam's bidding...

'I could take a look at it for you, if you like,' Caleb offered.

'Er—Cat usually sees to those sort of things,' Kate excused, giving Cat a slightly wary glance.

But she needn't have worried about Cat being offended by the offer. If the doorbell had broken yet again, Cat accepted that obviously she wasn't any better at maintaining the electrical appliances in this house than she was at cooking! Besides, this man, with all those letters he had after his name, should be able to fix a doorbell.

'Be my guest,' she invited. 'I'll get you the appropriate screwdriver and leave you to it. Then I'll be free to take Adam outside to the swings,' she added gleefully to the little boy, the widening of his grin enough to tell her he found this plan to his satisfaction. 'There you go.' She barely glanced at Caleb as she handed him the earthed screwdriver, reaching out for Adam's hand. 'To the swings!' she told the child excitedly, and they ran out of the house together and round to where the swings and slides were situated.

'Hello there, you two.' Kitty looked up from where she sat reading her book, her hair glowing golden in the early evening sunlight, blue eyes glowing with pleasure as she looked at Adam. 'A friend of yours, Cat?' she asked gently as he instantly hid behind Cat's legs.

'He certainly is.' Cat went down on her haunches beside the suddenly shy little boy, reminded of the nervous child she had met that first day. She hadn't realised that Kitty was outside in the garden—would have been even more annoyed at Caleb's familiarity if she had!—but as Kitty loved young children, and they usually took to her too, she was sure it wasn't going to be a problem. Besides, she and Kate had talked to Kitty about Adam, had known that she would understand...

'This is my new friend, Adam,' Cat introduced softly. 'Adam, this is another friend of mine. Her name is Kitty.'

'Have you met our cat yet, Adam?' Kitty enquired as their ginger tabby rubbed against her ankles. 'Her name is Madam Butterfly, but we call her Maddie for short.' She smiled encouragingly at the little boy as she leant down and carefully picked up the cat and cradled her in her arms. 'Maddie is going to have some baby kittens of her own very soon,' she added fondly.

This would be Maddie's second set of kittens in a year, but as they had had no trouble finding homes for her last litter they didn't envisage a problem with the next either. 'You'll have to come back and see them once they're born,' Cat told Adam, aware that time was passing. The last thing she wanted was for Caleb to come out into the garden in search of them. Toby might be completely ignorant when it came to opera, and particularly so when it came to Kitty's past fame, but Caleb had already shown that he wasn't...

Adam's face lit up at the thought of the kittens, making it easier for Cat to gently direct him away to the swings. He really was the most adorable child, she decided as she pushed him on the swing; his eyes were alight with pleasure and there were dimples in his thin cheeks as he smiled widely.

How sad that he had already known such unhappiness in his young life. He and Kitty had so much in common, she realised. Two kindred spirits...

'Penny for them?' Caleb murmured softly.

Cat gave a start, turning to him with annoyance; she had

been so concentrated on Adam, so deep in thought, she
hadn't even been aware of Caleb's approach across the garden.

She glanced quickly across to the rose garden where
Kitty had been sitting. Kitty had, as was usual when there
were people around that she didn't know, quietly disappeared back into her own suite of rooms inside the house.

Cat turned back to Caleb, smiling brightly now—probably more than was warranted if the way Caleb's eyes had
narrowed was anything to go by! 'Sometimes it's nice to
put your brain in neutral and just coast along for a while,'
she said breezily.

He nodded. 'Your doorbell is working again,' he informed her, taking over pushing Adam on the swing.

'Thank you.' She now felt a little shamefaced at the way
she had just left him to it.

Caleb shrugged. 'I'm glad I was able to be of help. I
was wondering...'

'Yes?' she prompted abruptly, instantly on the defensive,
wondering if he could have seen Kitty after all.

He looked at her steadily. 'I was wondering if you would
have dinner with me this evening.'

Cat couldn't have been more taken aback if he had suggested she take off all her clothes and dance naked around
the lawn!

'Me?' she squeaked, at once realising how ridiculous the
question sounded. And unsophisticated. As if men didn't
very often invite her out to dinner. But then, that was true...

To make matters worse, Caleb laughed at her obvious
surprise! Admittedly that laugh greatly improved his looks,
dispelling the arctic chill from his eyes, and his teeth very
white and even, dimples very similar to Adam's now visible beside his mouth. Although on a man in his late thirties
they were probably called laughter lines, Cat conceded
wryly.

'Sorry.' He sobered slowly, lips still quirked with humour. 'It just wasn't the usual reaction I get to a dinner invitation!'

She could well imagine that it wasn't! But, considering he had been a married man until six months ago, how many of these sort of invitations had he made lately?

'I'm just surprised *I'm* the person you're asking out to dinner,' she told him with her usual blunt honesty.

He raised one dark brow, lifting Adam down from the swing, the three of them walking back to the house now. 'As opposed to…?'

'Anyone!' She grimaced; they had seemed to antagonise each other from the word go!

Caleb chuckled softly. 'I like your honesty, Cat. One thing I can't stand in a woman is pretence,' he explained, a touch of bitterness in his voice now.

She gave him a searching look, but there was nothing to be read from his expression. Not that she had thought there would be. In his field of architectural history, Caleb was— quite literally!—an open book, as she had discovered at the library earlier this evening. As a father he was obviously caring and loving. But as a man—! Caleb Reynolds, the man, was an enigma. And not least because of his invitation to her!

She drew in a deep breath. 'In that case—'

'I saw the library books on the table in the hallway,' he put in quickly. 'Kate tells me they're yours?'

He knew damn well that she, with her 'honesty', had been about to turn down his dinner invitation! But by mentioning those books in the hallway he had put her in a defensive position. Architecture, especially the history of it, held no interest for her whatsoever, but she hadn't been able to resist borrowing two books by Caleb that she had found on the library shelves, intending to flick through them later this evening, curious in spite of herself. But she hadn't expected their author to see them and pass comment!

'Where do you intend taking me to dinner?' she returned challengingly.

'Would you believe, Rose Cottage? I don't have a babysitter for Adam this evening,' Caleb replied. 'Leaving him two evenings in a row would be too much.'

Of course it would. But dinner at his cottage? That was a bit much for a first date— *First date?* The description implied there might be a second one, and she doubted that very much. As Caleb had guessed all too easily last night, she didn't like him very much. But she was curious, she had to admit. Curious and intrigued.

'I think I'm wise to you, Caleb.' She gave a playful smile. 'You just want someone to cook dinner for you!' He was going to be very disappointed if he thought she would make anything like a good job of it!

'Not at all.' He shook his head. 'As it happens, I'm a pretty good cook myself. In fact, I'll put some potatoes in the oven to bake as soon as I get in; we can have them with a steak. If you would like to join me in an hour or so? That will give me time to bathe Adam and put him to bed.'

Very domesticated. Yet that was the last thing Caleb was! And just where in this conversation had she actually accepted his invitation?

'Fine,' she muttered, still grappling with the realisation that she had somehow agreed to have dinner at his cottage with him. What on earth were Kitty and Kate going to make of that? As for Toby—! Cat would make sure she had left before *he* arrived. The three of them could then spend the evening discussing her evening out with Caleb!

Caleb gathered up his son as soon as they were back in the kitchen. 'I'll see you in about an hour or so, then, Cat,' he told her briskly. 'I really ought to come back and pick you up. It's very ungentlemanly to expect you to drive yourself there.' He quirked mocking brows, obviously enjoying her discomfort as Kate looked at her sharply.

Cat felt sure this wasn't the first time the word 'ungentlemanly' had been levelled at him. Just as she was sure it didn't bother him one little bit what people thought of him! But with Kate looking on with suspicion she didn't intend getting into a discussion with him on the subject.

'I'll walk down,' she told him. 'It isn't far, and that way I'll be able to have a glass of wine with my meal. I'll bring a bottle of red with me. It will go nicely with the steak,' she added determinedly as she could see he was about to refuse her offer.

He could provide the food; he was probably a much better cook than she was—probably a much better everything than she was!—but she was still going to contribute to the meal in some way. And they had some rather nice bottles of red wine put by. Besides, she had a feeling she was going to need the wine to get her through the evening at all!

How on earth were two such unalike people as Caleb and herself going to spend an evening together? It was claimed that opposites attracted—but as far as Cat was aware attraction didn't come into this!

'Fine,' Caleb accepted without argument. 'Sorry to have interrupted your evening, Kate,' he apologised in parting.

Kate waited until he and Adam had left before turning to Cat with widely questioning eyes. 'Did I hear right?' she said slowly. 'Are you having dinner with Caleb Reynolds this evening?' She sounded as surprised as Cat had been when she'd received the invitation.

And with very good reason, Cat knew—she had only just finished telling Kate that she didn't like or trust the man! The truth of the matter was, she didn't like or trust any

man, had more than learnt her lesson five years ago—
Graham Barton had seen to that!

She shrugged. 'I realise it leaves you and Kitty to deal
with Toby—'

'Oh, don't worry about Toby,' Kate dismissed. 'I just—
You said you didn't like Caleb!'

Cat pulled a face. 'And I don't!' She held up her hands,
in self-defence. 'I have no idea how I came to be in the
position of having dinner with the man! Or why he should
have asked me in the first place…'

Kate laughed, an affectionately chiding laugh. 'Don't
you ever look in the mirror, Cat? Because if you did you
would see a rather lovely young lady, with glowing red
curls, huge green eyes surrounded by long dark lashes, and
the sort of pouting mouth I always wished for when I was
younger,' she said wistfully.

'Before you realised men prefer tall, willowy blondes?'
Cat returned humorously.

'Not all men—obviously,' Kate responded. 'Cat, do you
remember when we were little and we—?' She broke off,
looking as if her mind was far away. 'Sometimes all that
seems a very long time ago…!' she sighed.

'Wait until the two of you get to my age,' Kitty chided
affectionately as she joined them in the kitchen, putting an
arm around both their shoulders. 'That's the time to start
reminiscing. At your age, you're only just starting to make
your memories. Speaking of which…' She turned to Cat.
'I rather liked the look of your young man, Cat. He's very
handsome!'

'I—he—you—'

'Cat at a loss for words?' Kitty winked conspiratorially
at Kate as she straightened away from them both. 'She must
be smitten!'

'I most certainly am not!' Cat finally exploded indignantly. 'Caleb—the man you obviously saw out in the gar-

den with us—is Adam's father. And he isn't a young man,' she went on crossly. 'Nor mine—nor anyone else's from what I can gather. And as for being handsome—' She broke off suddenly, her face suffused with colour.

'Yes?' Kitty prompted with exaggerated innocence. 'That's twice in as many minutes that she's been rendered speechless,' she pointed out knowingly to Kate.

'Incredible,' Kate agreed conversationally, eyes glowing with laughter—at Cat's expense.

'Oh, give me a break, you two.' Cat turned away irritably. 'I'm not interested in Caleb Reynolds,' she denied forcefully—aware, even as she did so, that she was protesting too much.

But, really, she had only known the man three days, and— Then why, if she didn't find him attractive, did she have this slight fluttering sensation in the pit of her stomach just at the thought of spending the evening with him? Nerves; that was all it was, she told herself bracingly as she stamped out of the kitchen with the intention of changing for the evening ahead.

She walked through the hallway to get to the stairs, and there, face downwards, were those books of Caleb's that she had taken out at the library earlier.

Right, Mr Caleb Reynolds, she said firmly to herself as she picked up the books and took them to her bedroom with her. She might not know too much about him at the moment, but perhaps a quick look through his books would tell her a little more before she had to see him again this evening.

She had a feeling she was going to need all the advantages she could get!

CHAPTER FOUR

'OKAY.' Cat looked steadily at Caleb across the width of the small but cosy sitting-room of Rose Cottage. 'Do I call you Dr Reynolds or Professor Reynolds?'

Her quick glance through his books before coming here, enough of a glance to tell her she would read them through properly when she had more time—Caleb had a way of writing about architecture, especially the history of it, that piqued one's interest to know more—was also enough to tell her that those letters after his name entitled him to a much grander title than plain Mr!

She had enjoyed her stroll down to Rose Cottage, wearing a green sundress now in the warmth of the summer evening, happy as she'd listened to the birds singing in the trees, brightly coloured wild flowers growing on the roadside and in the hedges. It had been such a pleasant walk she had almost forgotten her destination was Rose Cottage and dinner with Caleb. Almost...

One look at him when he'd opened the door to her brief knock had been enough to set off that fluttering sensation in her stomach once again. He looked extremely male in the open-necked blue shirt and navy blue trousers he had changed into, freshly shaved and exuding the smell of a pleasant—and expensive, Cat felt sure!—aftershave.

Adam wasn't the only one to have taken advantage of the last hour to bathe. In fact, father and son might just have jumped into the bath together! It would certainly have been more efficient if they had, and Caleb struck Cat as a very efficient—and self-sufficient!—man.

Although thinking of him cavorting naked in the bath

had not been a good idea as soon as she'd set eyes on him again! Which was why she had turned the conversation to the subject of his work as soon as they were inside the cottage.

He gave a slow, leisurely smile, standing beside the unlit fireplace, looking down at her as she sat in an armchair—much as she had done to him on Sunday afternoon. 'I would prefer it if you just called me Caleb,' he drawled. 'And the title all depends on where I am, and who I'm with. With my colleagues I'm Dr Reynolds, to my students I'm Professor Reynolds. But I've also been known to answer to sir!' he informed her, grey eyes gleaming with laughter.

She would just bet he had! But he was going to be out of luck as far as she was concerned; they were well past the age when women were still subservient to men!

Although she was intrigued by the mention he had made of students. Teaching must be new to him, because it hadn't been documented in that biographical blurb in his book. 'Where do you teach?' she asked interestedly—his subject was obvious!

Caleb frowned slightly. 'Nowhere at the moment. I took a leave of absence after the accident six months ago,' he explained soberly.

The accident in which his wife had been killed, and Adam traumatised. 'I'm sorry,' Cat said softly.

'You've nothing to be sorry for,' Caleb dismissed harshly. 'There is plenty to regret about that day but—luckily for you—none of it was on your account.'

But plenty of it on his, if the bleakness of his expression was anything to go by. Cat couldn't help wondering—

'Enough of this doom and gloom,' Caleb announced suddenly, motivated into action. 'I have some white wine cooling outside as an aperitif.' He had taken the bottle of red from her when she arrived and put it in the kitchen. 'I suggest we go into the garden and have a glass.' He held the door open for Cat to precede him out of the cottage. 'It's such a lovely evening, I thought we could eat outside, if that's okay with you?'

It was a rhetorical question, Cat decided as they went out into the garden and she found the table there already set for their meal, right down to red candles in silver holders that could be lit as it got dark!

'You have been busy,' she observed wryly. All she had done in the last hour was withstand some teasing from Kate and Kitty, shower and change, before sitting down to look through this man's books. But, as she had guessed earlier, Caleb was extremely efficient. Even the wine was cooling in an ice-bucket placed beside the table!

His mouth twisted ruefully as he poured the two glasses of wine. 'I learned—the hard way!—when I took over the sole care of Adam six months ago that a single parent has to be extremely organised. For the first month—' he handed Cat one of the glasses of wine before sitting down next to her '—Adam and I lived in complete chaos. There seemed to be so much to do when I got out of bed in the morning that it seemed to be lunchtime before I even managed to get him washed and dressed. And as for mealtimes—!' He shook his head at the memory. 'Adam was very patient with me,' he said affectionately.

And, Cat guessed shrewdly, this man had been less so with himself. Loving children as she did, and with the training she had, the care of children came easily to her, but she could imagine that initially Caleb hadn't had a clue where to start. But he had managed, and now six months later, had everything under complete control, which was another indication of how determined he could be...

'This wine is delicious,' she told him absently, glancing around the garden. 'This is a lovely spot, isn't it?'

The cottage had once been part of the estate that belonged to Clive House, before the land was sold off, and the cottages in the village became either occupier-owned or were sold on to other people. This particular cottage had been bought originally by the grandmother of Jane Greenwood, the young girl who helped out at the play-school and who had babysat Adam the previous evening. But the elderly lady had died a couple of years ago, and her daughter, Jane's mother, had decided to keep the cottage and rent it out rather than sell it. Cat had a feeling it would one day be passed into Jane's hands, probably when she married.

The cottage itself was lovely, with its thatched roof, pristine white paintwork, and roses around the door—in keeping with its name. Bob Greenwood, Jane's father, was a keen gardener, and while the cottage was unoccupied he kept the garden as lovely as his own, the perfume from the abundance of flowers even now filling the night air.

It really was a beautiful spot, and the flowers' perfume was heady—unless it was the two or three sips of wine Cat had already taken? Whatever the cause, she could feel herself relaxing in the charm and intimacy of her surroundings. Which was not a good idea!

'I—'

'Will you excuse me a moment while I go inside and check on the food?' Again it was a rhetorical question, as Caleb suited his actions to his words.

Cat let out a sigh of relief. What was she *doing* here? More to the point, why had Caleb asked her here? The chilled wine, the candles on the table seemed to imply—

'Here we are.' Caleb came back into the garden, carrying a plate in each hand. 'I've cheated with our starters and desserts,' he announced without apology. 'Smoked salmon.' He put down the two plates, one on either side of the table. 'And we have strawberries for dessert. But I will be cooking the steaks myself,' he stated self-deprecatingly.

Cat had a feeling this man was more than capable of doing anything he set his mind to do!

The smoked salmon was beautifully arranged on the plates, with a wedge of lemon and a salad garnish, served with delicately thin brown bread and butter.

'I've never thought that cooking for yourself is an excuse to let standards drop,' he said as Cat stared at the food that any restaurant would have been proud to place before its customers.

After what she had said to Kate in their kitchen earlier, Cat felt a little shamefaced, but her 'standards' where food was concerned had simply never been this high. As a student she had been known to burn the baked beans that were going to be put on her undercooked toast! It wasn't that she didn't appreciate good food, she was just incapable of producing it for herself—or anyone else!

'This is— You can be chef if I ever decide to open a restaurant!' she told him as they sat down to eat.

He chuckled softly. 'The salmon came out of a packet, Cat,' he derided.

'It still wouldn't look like this if I had taken it out and put it on the plate,' she assured him.

'Cooking isn't your forte,' he replied understandingly.

Neither was squeezing the lemon wedge, she decided as it shot out of her hand, across the table, and landed on Caleb's plate. 'I'm not sure I've discovered what my forte is yet,' she admitted ruefully as he handed the lemon wedge back to her without comment.

'An affinity with children, if Adam's preference for you is anything to go by,' Caleb told her, his own lemon dealt with—without mishap, of course!—and disposed of on the side of his plate. 'I noticed that today he made a bee-line for you as soon as he arrived, and that he was with you again when I came to collect him at lunchtime.'

'He did play with the other children part of the morning,'

she defended, although she had to admit Adam had seemed to stay pretty close to her side for most of the morning. Although she didn't doubt that would change once he was more comfortable with the other children.

'I wasn't criticising, Cat,' Caleb assured her. 'It's wonderful that he's starting to relate to other people again. I think it's because you're able to meet him on his level,' he added thoughtfully.

Cat looked at him with laughter in her eyes. 'I'm not sure if I've just been complimented—or insulted!'

He returned her smile. 'I didn't say you go down to Adam's level, Cat,' he drawled. 'Just meet on the same level. Not too many adults have the ability to do that with any degree of success, for all that we're given the onerous task of guiding children into adulthood! It was a compliment, Cat,' he assured her huskily.

'In that case, thank you.'

'And may I add that I echo my son's discerning taste?' Caleb said gruffly.

No, he may not!

Cat's sudden interest in her food had nothing to do with the enjoyable freshness of the salmon, and much more to do with the fact that she was too disconcerted by Caleb's remark to even look at the man at the moment. What did he mean, he echoed his son's discerning taste—he didn't want to make a 'bee-line' for her too, did he?

On Sunday, he had seemed arrogant and cold, if not condescending, and a change to seductive admirer would be too much too suddenly! Why had he changed? Kate claimed it was because of what Cat should see herself every time she looked in the mirror, but Cat wasn't so sure...

'Cat—'

'Caleb, could we get one thing clear right now?' Cat cut in forcefully. 'No matter what opinion you may or may not have formed of me, I am not on the market for some brief, meaningless relationship that might keep you amused while you're in the area!' She was breathing deeply by the time she finished her outburst, her cheeks flushed with anger now rather than pleasure, her eyes the same deep emerald-green as her dress.

Caleb returned her gaze wordlessly for several long seconds, and then he studiously put down his knife and fork onto his plate before leaning his elbows on the table, linking his hands together and resting his chin on them. 'You're right, Cat, we should get a few things clear,' he murmured softly, eyes narrowed and unreadable. 'Firstly, no matter what opinion you may or may not have formed of *me*, I am not on the market for some brief, meaningless relationship that might keep you amused while I'm in the area, either! Secondly,' he continued firmly as she would have spoken, 'I have a three-and-a-half-year-old son asleep in the cottage, so if you think I can be seduced into bed later this evening forget it!'

Her mouth opened. And closed. And then opened and closed again. All without her having made a sound. Being rendered speechless three times in one day wasn't just incredible—it was unbelievable!

Caleb quirked mocking brows. 'Has no man ever turned you down before?'

'I wasn't going to ask!' She finally found her voice again. And not a minute too soon, either, from the way this conversation was going!

Caleb grinned at her outraged expression. 'Seduction isn't asking, Cat, it's exactly what it sounds like—gentle persuasion!'

'Gentle persuasion' with this man would be like using a cap-gun against a tank! 'I'm not into persuasion either,' she told him sharply. 'Gentle or otherwise!' She glared across the table at him.

'You know—' he relaxed back into his chair, calmly

returning her gaze '—I thought that about you on Sunday. I thought, There's a young lady who speaks her mind, be it tactful or not.'

'You told me you prefer honesty,' she reminded him tautly.

'Oh, I do,' Caleb agreed, still completely relaxed. 'It's much better to clear the air concerning these things, isn't it?'

'Clear the air'—they had bulldozed the subject!

'Were Kate and her grandmother okay about your coming out this evening?' He adeptly changed the subject as he gathered up their used plates.

'Fine,' Cat said breezily, on her guard again now. They might have cleared the air about the question of a relationship between the two of them, but that still left another: what was she doing here...? 'Toby was coming to dinner this evening, anyway,' she went on casually, having managed to avoid Toby earlier by leaving the house before he arrived.

But no doubt Toby would have something to say on the reason for her absence this evening the next time she saw him. In fact, Toby seemed to have something to say on most subjects. A bit like this man did!

Caleb looked at her with raised brows. 'He seems to be a regular visitor—you mentioned he had been to lunch with you on Sunday too,' he explained at Cat's puzzled look.

'Here, I'll help you with those.' She carried the side plates into the kitchen, a kitchen surprisingly tidy considering he was preparing dinner in it. But then, a lot about Caleb Reynolds surprised her! 'I think Toby visits us so much because he's bored,' she continued conversationally as Caleb began to grill the steaks. 'He moved here from London about a year ago, with visions of rural Bohemia, I think. But from the little he's said I gather he finds it too slow, and certainly not sophisticated enough for his city tastes. The most excitement we've had in the village in the last six months was when Mrs Thomas's Persian cat escaped his pampered luxury and Mrs Thomas had to chase him out into the road.'

Caleb looked across from watching the steaks under the grill. 'That was exciting?'

'Not the cat running out into the road.' Cat shook her head, eyes glowing deeply green as she grinned at him. 'But Mrs Thomas is in her mid-sixties,' she continued mischievously, 'and what she had forgotten, in her haste to recapture her cat, was that she was still in her nightgown! Normally that wouldn't have been a problem at seven-thirty in the morning, either,' she giggled. 'But Sam was just delivering the milk. And he still goes pale if anyone should mention Mrs Thomas in her sheer silk nightgown!'

The poor man had been so shaken by the sight of the overweight Vera Thomas running across the road in her see-through nightgown that by the time he reached Clive House Cat and Kate had had to invite him in for a cup of tea until his nerves settled!

'And Mrs Thomas now gets her milk in town,' she added humorously.

Caleb had started to chortle with the arrival of the milkman in her story, and now he laughed outright.

Cat's breath caught and held in her throat as he did so. The grey eyes were no longer cold but crinkled at the corners; his teeth were very white and even against his tanned skin. Caleb Reynolds, she decided in that minute, was gorgeous!

'And how is the cat?' Caleb asked once he had sobered.

'As spoilt as ever!' Cat returned with a smile.

'I noticed a slight lilt in your voice as you were talking of Mrs Thomas's dilemma; would that be an Irish accent I heard? I suppose with a name like Rourke it ought to be!'

'Sure an' 'tis Irish I be, right enuff, saw.' Cat spoke in

an exaggerated accent. 'I would be in serious trouble if my grandmother heard me speaking like that,' she admitted then in her normal voice. 'She spent years helping me to speak without the accent! Not that there's anything wrong with it.' She grinned. 'My father's accent is so strong that he can swear at one of his horses for a good five minutes or more without anyone understanding a word he's said!'

'Except the horses, presumably,' Caleb drawled mockingly.

'Oh, they understand him, all right,' Cat agreed. 'He isn't much taller than me, but he can gentle the wildest horse,' she told him with pride.

Caleb nodded, keeping an eye on the grilling steaks. 'I've heard of people that can do that. Do your family still live in Ireland?'

'My mother and father do,' she replied, suddenly realising she had been talking too much. Half a glass of wine, and her tongue was running away with her. Or else it was Caleb who was having that effect on her...

'No brothers or sisters?'

'Surprisingly, no.' She freely acknowledged the large families in Ireland. 'I think Dad would have liked a son, but it wasn't to be. And, unfortunately, I don't have his way with horses. I can ride, of course. In fact, I think I was put on a horse before I could walk. And before I could talk even! Horses are not my favourite animals,' she admitted at Caleb's questioning look. 'Unlike Dad, who thinks they're preferable to most people!'

'Rourke?' Caleb murmured consideringly. 'Your father wouldn't be Michael Rourke, would he, the jockey turned trainer?'

She *had* been talking too much! But how could she have guessed that a historian, a professor at that, would have a knowledge of horse racing, and trainers?

'The steaks,' she reminded him as she could see smoke

coming from behind him, grateful for the diversion. Although she had a feeling Caleb was a man who wouldn't be diverted for very long.

'Damn!' he cried as he pulled out the grill pan. 'I hope you like your steak well-done? At least, on one side!'

'Is there any other way to eat them?' Cat returned lightly. 'Do you have a salad I can prepare?' she offered helpfully. 'I feel pretty useless standing here doing nothing. And I'm quite safe with a salad.'

'In the fridge, already prepared,' Caleb told her as he dealt with the steaks. 'Although you can take it out to the table, if you like. I've already put the dressing on it,' he said as she took the bowl of appetising salad out of the fridge. 'There's also a bowl of sour cream and chives in there for the potatoes. And I have a pepper sauce for the steaks. I wasn't sure of your preferences,' he admitted as Cat looked across at him with raised brows. 'And my wife told me—often!—that I never did pay enough attention to other people's likes and dislikes,' he added hardly.

At a guess, Cat would have said it was his wife's likes and dislikes he had been blind to! She sensed a certain coolness between husband and wife, and wondered at the state of his marriage at the time of his wife's death...

But at least the burning steaks and the subsequent conversation had taken Caleb's attention from her family in Ireland, her father in particular. It wasn't a subject that was up for discussion. In fact, none of her family were...

'I like all of it,' Cat assured Caleb as they carried the food out into the garden.

'Good,' Caleb said, pouring red wine into their fresh glasses.

'I'll have a headache tomorrow. Mixing my wines,' she explained.

'The last thing you're going to need tomorrow, looking

after all those lively, noisy children,' Caleb conceded, once again seated opposite her.

'Except Adam, of course,' she said sadly, sipping the red wine. 'What's the long-term professional view on—on his condition?'

'The consensus seems to be that he'll talk again when he's good and ready. For his sake, I hope it's going to be sooner rather than later.'

In every other way that mattered, Adam was a normal child. He just wouldn't speak...

'Although,' Caleb continued drily, 'he's still managed to let me know he would like a kitten in the not too distant future!' He looked across at Cat with a pointedly raised brow.

'Ah.' She gave a perplexed frown. 'I don't think there was actually any mention of Adam having a kitten, only that he could come and see them after they were born,' she said slowly, trying to recall the exact conversation. 'He actually seemed more taken with Kitty.'

Caleb looked up from his steak. 'The expectant mother?'

Cat almost choked on her own steak. 'Kitty is Kate's grandmother,' she explained teasingly. 'And, at seventy-two, that particular description is doubtful—if not miraculous!'

He grinned at his own mistake. 'It's amazing what medical breakthroughs they're making nowadays!'

She giggled, shaking her head. 'I think that would be taking things a bit far!'

'I agree. So Adam met the mysterious Kitty earlier?'

Cat's good humour faded as quickly as it had appeared, and she eyed Caleb warily now. Had his invitation, the meal, the banter that accompanied it, all been leading to this point?

She could read nothing from Caleb's expression, but that very blandness was suspicious in itself; Caleb Reynolds was, she had discovered, a man of very definite ideas and attitudes, and bland was the last way she would ever have described any part of him!

'He met Kate's grandmother, yes,' she returned coolly, no longer enjoying her food, even though the steak, despite Caleb's misgivings, had turned out to be succulently delicious. In fact, she now wished the evening over.

'I would like to meet her some time, too,' Caleb said lightly, sipping his wine as he looked at Cat over the rim of his glass.

She was right to be wary of this man, she told herself. If she thought back over the evening, she had been coaxed into talking quite a lot about herself—more than she had done for quite some time!—and in return this man had told her absolutely nothing about himself. He hadn't even given her a straight answer to her opening question concerning his academic title!

'I'm sure that if you stay in the area long enough, Caleb, you will bump into Kitty some time,' she told him noncommittally. Because the meeting wouldn't be of her choosing, sure that if Caleb were to even see Kitty he would realise exactly who she was. And they had taken great pains to see that no outsiders should make such a discovery…

'I was hoping for a more formal introduction. Perhaps when you invite me to look round the house?'

Cat had been right to mistrust this man; she was sure of it now. All that talk about his great-great-grandfather—! Okay, so the relationship existed, but to her mind Caleb was far too pushy about wanting to see round the house— and about meeting Kitty.

'Perhaps,' she returned tautly. 'Although, as we've already explained to you, Kitty isn't too well at the moment.'

He met her gaze unblinkingly. 'She was well enough to meet Adam in the garden earlier— Okay, okay, Cat.' He held up pacifying hands as her mouth tightened in anger. 'I'm only winding you up.' He shook his head, his expression teasing now. 'If we're going to continue seeing each other, you're going to have to learn when I'm joking and when I'm serious.'

As far as Cat was concerned, they weren't 'seeing' each other now, let alone in the future. And as she didn't intend spending another evening alone with him like this—no matter what the provocation!—she had no need to 'learn' anything more about Caleb Reynolds. She didn't like him and, more importantly, she didn't trust him.

Not one little bit!

CHAPTER FIVE

'I THOUGHT,' Cat gasped as she attempted to move away from Caleb, 'that we had both agreed we weren't interested in a brief, meaningless relationship!'

He refused to release her, his arms like steel bands about her waist as he held her to the hardness of his body.

Cat had known he looked fit, muscles rippling beneath his shirt, but she still hadn't been prepared for the strength of him minutes ago when he had first taken her into his arms!

By the time they'd finished their meal, and despite the flickering candles, it was quite dark, and becoming a little cool, and Cat had welcomed Caleb's suggestion that they move into the cottage. She had looked on the suggestion as one step closer to her making her excuses and leaving for home! What she hadn't expected, once they were in the cosy lounge of the cottage, was that Caleb would take her in his arms and kiss her. And not just a light kiss either, but a merging of their lips, a moulding of their bodies that took Cat's breath away.

At least, that was the excuse she gave herself when she finally managed to pull back a little in his arms...

She had been kissed before—of course she had, had had her fair share of boyfriends when she was at college. But none of them had made her feel the way Caleb did... His mouth had been firm and yet caressing, his arms strong about her waist, but his hands a gentle caress on her back. As the kiss had deepened and lengthened, she had felt the heat of excitement coursing through her. But it had been a feeling of panic at the emotions he was arousing that had made her pull back from him moments ago.

Caleb looked down at her now, his face only inches away from her own. His eyes were a deep smoky grey, and there was the flush of his own surging emotions on the hard planes of his cheeks. 'I've paid for an initial rental of Rose Cottage for six months,' he told her gruffly, 'which rules out "brief", don't you think? And no relationship can be called "meaningless" until you go along with it and see where it's going to take you!'

Where this particular relationship would take her was into Caleb's arms and the pleasure of his kisses! And that could only spell disaster. For everyone.

'Caleb—'

'Cat.' He put gently silencing fingertips against her lips, lashes long and dark as he looked at her with those smoky grey eyes. 'We've enjoyed a relaxed meal together, indulged in the customary goodnight kiss; let's leave it at that, hmm?'

No, she couldn't leave it at that! Because his way left it open for them to spend other evenings together like this. After the pleasure she had known in his arms a few minutes ago, she couldn't allow that...

This time she had no difficulty in pulling out of his arms. Because he allowed her to do so, she acknowledged, his arms dropping lightly down to his sides. She inwardly berated herself for her brief feeling of loss. She hardly knew the man; how on earth could she be feeling the loss of his closeness in this way?

'Caleb—'

'Much as I would like to keep you here with me longer—' he smoothly cut in on her protest '—I'm aware that it's late, and that you have a job of work to do in the morning. But I still find it irksome that I can't see you home.' His face showed his irritation at the fact.

Cat gave a dismissive shake of her head. 'As long as Mrs Thomas's cat hasn't escaped again, I should be safe from any unwanted surprises!' she assured him. 'It's a bright moonlit evening, Caleb; I'm sure I shall be perfectly okay walking the short distance home,' she added slightly impatiently as he still looked unhappy.

'Nevertheless, I would still appreciate it if you could give me a quick ring when you get in——'

'You're being ridiculous now, Caleb,' she snapped—it sounded too much like a shared intimacy, an exaggeration of their relationship, for her to telephone him as soon as she got in, just to let him know she was safe!

'Maybe. And maybe not.' His tone was inflexible. 'I would still appreciate the phone call.'

And she would 'appreciate' him not being so damned—

'I could always call you,' he suggested mildly.

And wake the whole household up by doing so. Wonderful!

'Perhaps not,' he conceded at her disgusted expression. 'Look, if it makes you feel better,' he continued, 'I won't even pick up the receiver. Just let it ring three times, and I'll know it was you.'

Who else would it be ringing him at almost eleven-thirty at night? Besides, 'three rings' also sounded—

'For God's sake, woman!' Caleb gave a rueful laugh at what Cat knew to be her scowling expression. 'Just pick up the phone and ring, damn it!'

'Yes—sir, wasn't it?' she came back tartly, reminding him of their conversation earlier this evening.

His eyes still laughed at her. 'It will do—until you can think of something better to call me!'

She could think of plenty of things to call this man— and at this moment 'sir' was the politest of them! 'Three rings,' she muttered in agreement, turning to leave.

'No polite ''thank you'' for dinner?' Caleb followed her

out into the hallway, out through the door, and down the garden path to the gate.

Cat turned to look at him, at the cottage she had admired so much earlier for its rustic charm. There was no doubting that the setting was idyllic, but the man standing in front of her was far from that—he didn't belong here, either at the cottage or in the village. And she had to keep remembering that. Because the village was her home, and would continue to be so long after this man had gone...

Her lips curled mockingly. 'I thought that was included in the "customary goodnight kiss"!'

He grinned in the moonlight. 'So it was.'

'Well...if there's nothing else...?'

'I can think of plenty else, Cat,' he responded at her barely concealed sarcasm. 'But it'll keep. Take care walking home. And don't forget the three rings,' he reminded her warningly. 'I would hate to disturb the whole household by ringing you just because you're too stubborn to do as I asked!'

He would, too, Cat accepted with annoyance. Damn him. One dinner together, even the indulgence of the 'customary goodnight kiss', did not give him the right—

'I see someone has thoughtfully left some lights on for you.' Caleb gestured in the direction of Clive House where it could clearly be seen about a quarter of a mile away, a light left on outside, another glowing in the kitchen. 'Nice to know I'm not the only one being ridiculous,' he told her with satisfaction.

Cat gave an impatient sigh before stepping out onto the pavement. ''Night, Caleb,' she told him abruptly.

'We'll arrange things differently from this next time,' he promised softly as she walked away.

Cat didn't even hesitate in her determined strides home. Next time! There wouldn't be a next time, not for the two of them! She had been cajoled and then coerced into accepting this evening's invitation, but she would be much more on her guard around Caleb Reynolds in future. He was a man used to getting his own way. And as she was a woman accustomed to doing exactly as she pleased the two of them were completely incompatible.

Except for that kiss they had shared...

She couldn't deny they had been more than compatible then; in fact they had seemed to fit together like two halves of a whole, their passion melding as perfectly as their bodies had moulded together. Cat could still feel the warm responsiveness of Caleb's mouth against hers, the caress of his hands down her spine, that— No! She couldn't become involved with Caleb. She just couldn't!

Cat was surprised to see Kate was still up, drinking coffee in the kitchen, when she let herself into the house ten minutes after leaving Caleb. 'I thought you would have gone to bed hours ago,' she greeted warmly.

Kate returned her warmth. 'You go out to have dinner with the fascinating Caleb Reynolds—and you expect me to go to bed without hearing all the details of the evening?' She shook her head, blue eyes glowing teasingly.

'He isn't fascinating,' Cat clipped with a scowl, moving to the telephone to flick through the book they always kept beside it, listing, amongst a lot of others, the names and telephone numbers of all the parents of the children they looked after. 'A lot of other things,' she told her friend firmly as she picked up the receiver and pressed the appropriate buttons. 'But fascinating certainly isn't one of them!'

'Who on earth are you telephoning at this time of night?' Kate looked astounded by the lateness of her call.

'Don't ask!' she muttered, listening to the dialling tone; one, two—

'Hello, Cat,' Caleb greeted huskily before it could ring for the third time.

'You said you wouldn't pick up the receiver!' She spluttered her indignation. 'You promised,' she went on accusingly.

'I may have said I wouldn't, but I certainly didn't promise,' he reasoned. 'But, even if I had, I would have had my fingers crossed behind my back at the time!'

'You—you— Next time I want your hands—both of them!—in full view when we make any sort of agreement!' Next time? She was doing it too now! There wouldn't *be* a next time!

'That's fine with me, Cat,' he agreed smoothly. 'I'll see you in the morning. Sweet dreams, love.' He rang off.

Cat still grasped the receiver, couldn't seem to move. He had called her 'love'. Coming from him it had certainly sounded like an endearment! He couldn't go around calling a virtual stranger 'love'. He—

'I should put the receiver down, Cat, dear,' Kate advised gently after several seconds. 'There's obviously no one on the end of the line now. Caleb?' she prompted as a still dazed Cat put down the receiver and dropped down into the chair opposite hers at the kitchen table.

'Caleb,' she acknowledged heavily.

Kate's eyes widened. 'Sounds like you had an interesting evening…?'

Interesting? It hadn't been interesting! Awkward. Uncomfortable. Tense. Teasing. That kiss rapturous. But it hadn't been interesting!

She gave a heavy sigh. 'I've just spent three hours in that infuriating man's company, and do you know what I realised on my walk back home? I know nothing more about him now than I did before I went out.' She angrily answered her own question.

She had gone over their conversation in her head as she'd walked back, finding the journey in the darkness more unnerving than she had believed possible—or would ever ad-

mit to!—and as she had done so she had realised, apart
from the fact that she had learned he sometimes taught his
specialist subject, she knew nothing else about him, not
about his life before he moved here, and certainly not about
his marriage. Considering the way he had encouraged her
to talk about herself, and her family, she found that extremely odd...

'How was your evening?' she asked Kate, attempting to
shake off her feelings of misgiving.

'Oh, no, you don't!' Kate protested laughingly. 'We all,
and I do mean all, want to know how your evening went.
In fact, we spent the majority of the evening speculating
about it!' she admitted ruefully.

'One—or all of you!—could have come down and seen
for yourself,' Cat grumbled. 'I would have welcomed the
interruption!' Especially during the last half an hour, when
Caleb had kissed her.

'And Caleb, I'm sure, would have viewed it as an intrusion,' Kate said mischievously at Cat's scowl. 'Oh, come
on, Cat, it can't have been that bad!'

It hadn't been bad at all; in fact, when she had accompanied Caleb to check on Adam, an Adam who'd looked
even more angelic than usual curled up asleep in his bed,
blond hair lightly brushing his brow, she had been filled
with a warm, protective glow towards the little boy. She
had also realised in that moment that she was becoming
unprofessionally fond of Adam... And that was an emotion
she didn't want to feel towards his father!

'I'm not sure it's ethically correct to have dinner with
the parent of one of the children in our care,' Cat said.

Kate seemed unconcerned. 'We've been to several bar-
becues given by parents.'

'Single parent, then. As in father of.' Cat made her point
plain, although she knew Kate well enough to know her
friend was already well aware of exactly what she meant.

'It isn't as if there's a mother, too,' Kate reasoned gently. 'Then it would definitely be unethical. As well as stupid!'

Cat wasn't convinced. 'I still think it would be a mistake to allow him too close.'

'To us? Or to you?'

'Both!'

'Is that what you did?' Kate probed quietly.

'No, of course not,' Cat instantly denied, aware that as she did so she couldn't quite meet Kate's sympathetically questioning gaze.

'Well, that's okay, then, isn't it?' Kate insisted. 'And, to answer your earlier question, our evening was just fine. We had a very nice meal; in fact it was so nice that we decided to eat outside.'

'So did we. It was a lovely, warm evening,' Cat rejoined defensively, inwardly berating herself for again referring to her evening with Caleb; the less said about it the better! 'How was Toby?'

Her friend shrugged. 'His usual outrageous self,' she sighed. 'But Kitty enjoys his company.'

Kitty always did; it was one of the reasons they allowed him so much freedom when it came to his visits here. For all that she never talked about it, Kitty had to miss the glamour and excitement she had once known in her career, and Toby, with his years spent living in London, and his sophisticated humour, always managed to make her laugh. The two of them spent hours together just talking about places in London they were both familiar with, and although Toby had no idea Kitty was Katherine Maitland— her career and worldwide success had been just a bit before his time—he obviously enjoyed his visits too.

'Probably because he isn't always trying to persuade her into bed the way he is us!' Cat exclaimed disgustedly. 'And talking of bed...' She stood up decisively. 'As I have al-

ready been reminded once this evening, we have a job of
work to do in the morning.'

'A concerned parent?' Kate said, amused, switching off
the light to follow Cat from the room.

'An arrogant one!' Cat returned pointedly, absently wondering if Caleb had now noticed the switching off of the
kitchen light; she had never realised before tonight that
Clive House could be seen from Rose Cottage.

But as she stood in her still darkened bedroom several
minutes later, looking out of the window, she realised she
could see Rose Cottage quite clearly too. Even as she
watched, the light in the cottage's kitchen was switched off,
one flicking on upstairs seconds later in the bedroom that
faced in Clive House's direction. She could vaguely see the
shape of someone moving about the room, that figure moving to the window too now, a hand being raised before the
curtains were pulled across like a screen.

Caleb...

She didn't believe in coincidences any more where this
man was concerned, was sure Caleb had waited until he
saw their kitchen light go off before going up to bed himself. His lifting of his hand in a goodnight gesture seemed
to confirm that.

As she lay in bed some time later, finally having turned
off her bedside lamp, the moonlight streaming in through
her bedroom window, she couldn't help but remember the
husky warmth with which Caleb had wished her 'sweet
dreams, love'...

'So who is this Caleb Reynolds?' Toby demanded darkly.

Cat had asked herself the same question several times
today!

Caleb had dropped Adam off this morning with barely a
glance in her direction, let alone any word of greeting,
seeming preoccupied with his own thoughts. Unless, like

her, he was wondering what had happened between them last night, and was back-pedalling as fast as she was. She could only hope that was the case!

There had been no chance for him to talk to her when he'd come back to collect Adam at twelve-thirty, Cat had been busy supervising lunch for the children that stayed with them all day, and Kate had been the one to deal with Adam's departure. She hadn't mentioned anything about Caleb when she and Cat got together later.

The last person Cat had expected, or hoped, to see, as she'd walked to the post office-cum-village store later that afternoon, was Toby. And his opening remark was exactly the reason she was in no hurry to see him again!

She smiled up at him, the sunshine giving a red glow to her curls, her arms and legs tanned a golden brown against the yellow sundress she wore. That smile she gave Toby was as much for Lilley Stewart's benefit as it was for Toby's; the other woman was watching their exchange from the shop window with avid interest, no doubt aware— in a community as small as this one, it was inevitable!— that Cat had been to dinner at Rose Cottage the previous evening!

'Strange,' she lightly taunted Toby, 'he asked the same thing about you!'

Toby's expression deepened to petulance; he was dressed scruffily as usual, paint on his tee shirt, his denims old and faded. 'What does he do, Cat?'

'He's a Professor of History,' she told him. 'And he's doing some sort of work at the museum in York at the moment.' Although she was sure Kate or Kitty must have told Toby at least this much the evening before!

'Never heard of him,' Toby dismissed.

'Funny, he said that about you too,' Cat returned drily.

Toby gave her a look of exasperated impatience. 'This isn't funny, Cat—'

shopping to do.' She brushed past him and went into the shop, hoping Lilley would think the red in her cheeks was from the heat of the day and not temper—as it most assuredly was! How dared Toby talk to her in that—that possessive way, almost as if he had some claim on her? Which he most certainly did not!

'Lovely day again, isn't it, Cat?' Lilley greeted her, a woman in her mid-fifties who, lovely day or bad, habitually wore a neat woollen jumper and tweed skirt. Today was no exception, despite the warm summer weather.

'Lovely,' Cat agreed breezily. 'In fact, that's why I'm here; we thought we might have a salad for tea, and I've come down for some of your delicious home-cooked ham. Six slices should do it.'

'Warm enough to eat outside again this evening, isn't it?' Lilley chatted conversationally as she sliced the ham on the machine.

Again, Cat noted ruefully, maybe she wasn't the only one who could see across to Rose Cottage...?

'As long as you manage to avoid the bugs,' Cat rejoined cheerfully, refusing to be drawn by the 'again'.

'I was just saying to Mr Westward,' Lilley said, wrapping up the ham, 'we seem to be inundated with them this year.'

Mr Westward, Cat noted with amusement. The women were all addressed by Lilley by their first names, but any man who came into the shop was always called Mr. As a spinster, perhaps Lilley thought she was safer avoiding familiarity where men were concerned!

Cat shrugged dismissively. 'I hadn't really noticed.' And she hadn't; her remark about the bugs had merely been an avoidance of the 'again' in Lilley's earlier remark.

'Anything else I can get for you?' Lilley enquired brightly, her eyes gleaming with curiosity behind glasses that were always perched on the end of her nose.

'Kate mentioned we were getting short of coffee,' Cat said in reply.

'I can never drink coffee last thing at night,' Lilley chattered on as she turned to get the jar of instant coffee off the shelf behind her. 'I find it keeps me awake. How about you?' She looked across at Cat unblinkingly.

As Lilley was probably very well aware, her bedroom light had remained on very late last night—and her insomnia had had nothing to do with drinking coffee!

'Not that I've noticed,' Cat returned noncommittally once again, deciding at that moment that Kate would be the one to come down to the shop the next time they needed something; she was confused enough herself about last night, and even more so since Caleb's coolness earlier today, without having to fend off Lilley's questions.

'I see we have a new tenant at Rose Cottage.' Lilley, obviously having noticed Cat reaching for her purse so that she could pay for her goods, quickly moved on to the subject that really interested her. 'A gentleman from London. A Mr Reynolds. I expect he'll be a friend of yours?'

This last question was, to say the least, ambiguous—deliberately so, Cat felt. Did Lilley mean Caleb was a friend of hers now, or did she mean had Caleb been a friend of hers before he came to the village? The truthful answer, to either question, was no. She might have spent the previous evening having dinner with him, but she certainly wouldn't call him a friend. She wasn't sure what he was...

'No,' she answered with brevity. 'Although his son comes to playschool.'

'Such a lovely little boy,' Lilley reflected. 'Although he doesn't seem to say much.'

Of course Adam didn't say anything at all, but that didn't mean that Cat was about to get into a conversation with Lilley about him either! It wasn't that Lilley was malicious in her interest, because she wasn't; in fact she was a very likeable woman; she just had to know what was going on. But Caleb hadn't given the impression he liked to be talked about, no matter what the circumstances.

'Adam's just shy, Lilley,' Cat said tactfully, handing over her money before turning to leave. 'Give him a few weeks to get over his shyness, and he'll be as talkative as—'

'His father?' Lilley put in, obviously still hopeful of learning something.

Caleb was about as talkative as a clam! 'As the other children,' Cat concluded firmly. 'Have a pleasant evening, Lilley,' she called in parting.

It was definitely Kate's turn to come down to the shop next time. No doubt Lilley would take great delight in questioning her about Toby!

But it *was* a lovely evening, the sort of hot summer day in England that brought a lift to the spirits, and a smile to one's lips, the sort of evening when—

'Like a lift home?'

The sort of evening when Caleb, with a smiling Adam strapped into the back of his car, stopped—in full view of the post-office window!—and offered her a lift home!

CHAPTER SIX

CAT stared at Caleb through the space made by the electronic lowering of the car window. What were the chances—?

Not too high, she would have thought. And as Lilley's head was bobbing up and down in the shop window she obviously agreed with that!

Caleb looked up at Cat sardonically. 'It's only a lift, Cat,' he drawled at her hesitation. 'Not a life-changing decision!'

To him it was a lift, but he would eventually leave the village, whereas Cat—

'A lift home, Cat,' Caleb repeated. 'See—both hands on the steering-wheel,' he added tauntingly.

She shot him an irritated glare before walking around the back of the car and getting in the passenger side. 'That was a sneaky move of yours last night,' she hissed at him before turning to smile warmly at Adam. 'Have you had a nice afternoon?' she enquired of the little boy gently, his response an enthusiastic nod.

'I took him for a swim at the local pool,' Caleb explained as he put the car in gear and accelerated away from the shop.

Much to Cat's relief! Lilley's nose had actually been pressed against the window in an effort to see what was going on outside, and Cat didn't want to give her any more scope for speculation. If she needed any! Firstly Cat had stopped to talk to Toby outside the shop, and now Caleb had stopped and was giving her a lift home. By sunset tonight it would be all over the village that she was involved with both men!

It was like this at home in Ireland too, of course, but after spending three years away at college she'd found it a little difficult to slot back into a small and close community—especially the accompanying gossip.

'It's a pity you couldn't have come with us, but I appreciate you had to work this afternoon,' Caleb continued.

After his coolness towards her this morning, she doubted she would have accepted the invitation anyway! 'That's right, Professor,' she returned tartly.

He gave her a surprised sideways glance. 'You aren't one of my students, Cat.'

'I thought "sir" was going a little too far,' she came back tautly.

'Have I done something to upset you, Cat?' He slowed the car down as they approached her home. 'Which sneaky move were you referring to?' he asked as he stopped the car, switching off the engine before turning in his seat to look at her fully, his hand resting along the back of her seat, those long fingers starting to play with the fiery curls at her nape.

Picking up the telephone last night when he had said he wouldn't, or minutes later waving to her from his bedroom window? She didn't really want to get into a discussion about either of those things.

She wished he wouldn't play with her hair like this; it was very difficult to concentrate on anything when his fingers were lightly caressing against her skin, when that light caress was causing a tingling sensation that spread over her shoulders and back.

She swallowed hard, trying to remember what he had just said to her, let alone why she had been annoyed with him in the first place. Oh, yes, she remembered now...

'You weren't exactly friendly this morning—'

Caleb's softly teasing laughter cut in on her admonition. 'Oh, Cat, little Cat.' He shook his head in mock-exasperation. 'I did that for you. I thought it best, with all those mothers looking on. I didn't think you'd want me to give them anything to gossip about.'

Now it was Cat's turn to laugh. Not give them anything to gossip about! This man had no idea of village life—he really didn't!

'I think you're a little late with your concern about the gossip,' she told him drily.

Dark brows rose over gleaming grey eyes. 'Courtesy of Lilley at the post office again?'

'In one,' Cat confirmed, getting out of the car. 'Would the two of you like to come in for a cup of tea? I'm sure Kate would love to see you both,' she found herself asking as Caleb got out of the car.

'Kate would like to see us both?' he murmured close to Cat's ear before bending down to unstrap Adam from the back of the car.

Cat avoided his eyes as he straightened, wishing it didn't show so much when she blushed. But with this red hair, and freckled complexion, what chance did she have of that?

Instead of answering Caleb's mockery, she turned to Adam, holding out her hand towards him. 'I have a surprise for you, Adam,' she told him excitedly. 'Can you guess what it is?'

'Whatever it is—' Caleb reached out and took hold of her other hand as his son looked up at her in anticipation '—I want to come too!'

This was ridiculous!

Men had played little part in her life the last few years, most of her time and energy concentrated, as were Kate's, on making a success of their playschool. She had been out on the odd date here and there, but none of those men had made the slightest impression on her, and for the last six months Toby had been the only male company any of them had had. Yet Caleb only had to touch her and she felt a quivering warmth coursing through her body.

Why him? That was what she wanted to know. She wasn't even sure whether she liked him or not, and he certainly wasn't comfortable to be with. But that warm pleasure inside her seemed to increase as he refused to let go of her hand.

'It's Adam's surprise,' she told him firmly. 'You're only here because he is,' she added tartly, relieved to have that tingling sensation in her hand cease as he slowly let her go. It was inexplicable. It was unacceptable. It was unbearable!

His gaze openly laughed at her before he turned to Kate as they entered the kitchen. 'I hope we aren't intruding?' He was at his most charming as he apologised for interrupting the mixing of the cake Kate was obviously in the middle of baking.

Cat's breath caught sharply in her throat at his deliberate mockery, and Kate gave her a teasing look of acknowledgement to let her know she had overheard her last remark to Caleb just before they'd entered the kitchen together.

'Not in the least,' Kate answered him as charmingly, wiping her hands on the towel. 'I was just about to make a pot of tea; would you like a cup?'

'How nice.' Caleb shot Cat a mocking glance. 'Unless Cat has something else to do?'

'As a matter of fact, I do,' Cat told him with satisfaction. 'Adam and I are going to see Maddie and her kittens!' She squeezed the little hand conspiratorially as Adam's face lit up with pleasure. 'She had four, Adam.' Cat went down on one knee beside him. 'But they're only a few hours old, so we have to be very quiet and not disturb any of them. And we can't stay long either, because Maddie is very tired. But I know you would like to see them.' She brushed back a blond curl from the smoothness of his brow, once again convinced he must have got this blond hair and brown eyes from his mother, although his features were definitely miniatures of his father's. And, unlike his father, Adam had already found a place in her heart…

'I'll have some juice waiting for you,' Kate promised Adam encouragingly.

'I take it I'm not invited to join you,' Caleb accepted drily before sitting down at one of the chairs at the kitchen table. 'So I'll stay here and keep Kate company.'

Cat led the little boy further into the house. Caleb wasn't invited for two reasons: firstly, because this was something special for Adam, and secondly because Maddie had chosen to give birth in a basket in Kitty's private sitting-room!

Kitty's sitting-room was totally personal to herself, family photographs everywhere, some of them clearly of Katherine Maitland at the height of her career. Plus later ones with Kate as a baby, and then other ones of their years in Ireland. While they would mean absolutely nothing to Adam, the same couldn't be said of his father!

Kitty was still in her bedroom taking her afternoon rest, but Cat and Adam were very quiet, neither of them wanting to disturb the new mother and her tiny kittens. And they were adorable kittens, only about three inches long, with the tiniest little faces, so young their eyes were still closed. There were two ginger tabbies like their mother, another with ginger, black and white markings, and another one black with white paws. Their paternity was impossible to even guess at, Cat thought affectionately, but Maddie obviously adored her new offspring, constantly washing them as she and Adam watched.

The new mother looked up at the two human beings who had come to view her new family, seeming almost to smile her pride before she once again began to wash her babies.

Cat looked at Adam's face as he gazed down at them, emotion catching in her throat at the wonderment in his face. When he looked up at her, there were tears in his eyes. 'They're lovely, aren't they?' she whispered. 'Your daddy says you might like one of your own once they're big enough to leave their mother.' She didn't think she was speaking out of turn by mentioning Caleb's comment.

But Adam's reaction to it was completely unexpected as he recoiled away from her as if she had struck him, his eyes wide with shock and horror.

'Adam...?' she gasped questioningly. But before she could stop him he turned on his heel and ran out of the sitting-room back towards the kitchen.

Cat followed more slowly, totally dazed by his behaviour. He had been excited about the kittens Maddie was expecting, had even indicated to his father that he would like one, and he had seemed absolutely entranced by the tiny creatures just now. So what had she done or said that had caused him to react so violently? She went back over their conversation, and as she did so she realised exactly what she had said to alarm Adam; she had told him the kittens would one day be big enough to leave their mother...!

She had no idea what Caleb's relationship with his wife had been like before the accident, had no idea of the circumstances behind that accident, although she did remember Caleb saying there were things to regret about that day—and she had the feeling he hadn't been referring to the fact that his wife had died. From Adam's reaction just now, Cat had a feeling that one of those regrets had something to do with Adam being with his mother when the accident occurred.

Did Caleb realise that Adam, in some inexplicable way, felt a responsibility for his mother's death...?

Because after his reaction to the news that the kittens would be taken away from Maddie, Cat now had the feeling it was all tied up with Adam's relationship with his own mother. Of course her death had been traumatic, as had been in the car with her when it happened, but Adam's lack of speech seemed to point at some deeper scar even than those.

She had to talk to Caleb.

For all that they had spent an enjoyable evening together last night—she refused to think about that kiss!—and for all that he seemed relaxed and charming in their company, she had the distinct feeling that wouldn't be the case if she tried to talk to him about something he felt was too personal. The circumstances behind his wife's death could certainly be classed as that!

Oh, well, fear of rebuke for interfering had never stopped her before. As it wouldn't now...

Adam was sitting on his father's knee drinking juice when Cat got back to the kitchen, his face deliberately turned away from her, it seemed. However, from the way the conversation between Kate and Caleb was flowing around him, he hadn't transferred his distress to either of them.

He kept his face averted as Cat sat down to drink the cup of tea Kate had poured for her. She had lost him, Cat realised painfully. He had betrayed some of his inner pain to her, and now he couldn't forgive her for that.

'Is Kitty awake?'

Cat turned to Kate. 'I didn't see her.'

Kate gave her friend a searching look, obviously wondering then at Cat's own delay in returning from viewing the kittens. Cat gave a barely perceptible shake of her head, sipping her tea, while at the same time very aware of accusing brown eyes suddenly turned in her direction.

Adam didn't trust her any more.

It hurt, she couldn't say that it didn't, the partiality he had shown for her up till now more than returned. But she knew that after today he was more likely to want to avoid her altogether.

'Well, thank you for the tea, ladies.' Caleb spoke into the silence several minutes later, standing up, putting Adam down as he did so, the little boy instantly moving slightly behind his father's legs, as he had on Sunday when they had met him for the first time. 'Time we were going home to cook dinner,' Caleb said.

'You could—'

'Time we were doing something about ours too,' Cat cut in lightly on what she was sure was Kate's invitation for father and son to join them for their evening meal. It was only salad and ham, as she had told Lilley earlier, and there would be plenty for all of them, but Cat really couldn't bear to watch Adam's squirming any longer. 'Thank you for driving me home, Caleb,' she said politely.

He looked at her with narrowed eyes, obviously also aware of the invitation she had put a stop to. 'You're welcome,' he bit out abruptly.

She nodded tersely. 'I'll walk you to the door.'

'Cat—'

'I won't be long, Kate,' she told her companion firmly, accompanying Caleb and Adam not just to the front door, but outside to the car too.

'Making sure we're off the premises, Cat?' Caleb taunted as he straightened from putting Adam safely in the back of the car.

'I need to talk to you, Caleb,' she told him quietly, not wanting Adam to hear her, aware that he was still watching her anxiously.

Caleb's face tightened warily. 'Concerning what?'

She glanced at Adam again, tears of frustration and pain in his eyes now. 'Could I come down to the cottage later, once Adam is asleep?' She kept her voice low.

Dark brows rose over icy grey eyes. 'This is so sudden, Cat—'

'Please don't try and be funny, Caleb,' she snapped fiercely, eyes flashing deeply green. 'Something happened earlier. I—' She glanced at Adam again. That he was agitated she didn't doubt, could clearly see that he was by the way he plucked at his seat belt with nervous fingers. She didn't want to make things worse for him, but she could see that to his young mind she already had! 'I'll be down about nine o'clock,' she told Caleb firmly.

He gave a mocking inclination of his head. 'It seems I have little choice in the matter,' he drawled.

Cat gave an impatient sigh. 'This isn't the time for games, Caleb,' she bit back, shooting Adam another concerned look; the last thing she wanted him to think was that they were in some way united against him! To her mind, the situation was bad enough already, without that.

'Obviously not.' Caleb conveyed his puzzlement at her behaviour. 'Nine o'clock,' he confirmed tersely.

'Oh, and Caleb.' She hurriedly stopped him before he could open the car door and so make it possible for Adam to overhear their conversation. 'Whatever you do,' she warned as Caleb paused with his hand on the door handle, 'don't tell Adam I'm coming to the cottage later. And don't mention the kittens to him!' she implored.

'Don't...?' Caleb's puzzlement deepened. 'I haven't a clue what's going on, but I'm sure you'll explain it all to me very shortly,' he added with pointed impatience.

'I think it may be a case of *your* explaining a few things to me,' Cat told him heavily—namely, how on earth a three-year-old child could possibly think he was responsible, in any way, for the death of his mother! And why the little boy had recoiled in horror at the thought of the kittens being taken away from their mother...

She looked at Caleb with narrowed eyes, several conclusions already being drawn in her own mind as to the possible answer to that last question. Caleb's voice cooled noticeably whenever his wife was mentioned, and he had already admitted to regrets about the day she died. Could one of those regrets possibly have been an argument over Adam? An argument Adam had overheard...?

She didn't actually know the real answer to those questions. But she was sure that Caleb did. And, although he might not like it, for Adam's sake, there might be things Caleb would have to talk about later this evening that he would consider none of her business. Which, she accepted, they probably weren't. But she wanted to help Adam...

She didn't even stop to consider what her interference in his personal business might do to her own relationship with Caleb. It had barely begun, anyway, she told herself, and would ultimately lead nowhere. Except possibly to heartache. Besides, Adam was the one who was important now.

Caleb's mouth tightened as he read, but didn't understand, the determination in her gaze. 'Nine o'clock,' he reaffirmed tersely before getting into the car and driving off without a second glance.

Cat noted with regret that tonight there was no eager-faced Adam looking out of the back window. The tenuous bond they had formed over the last few days had been wiped out, and by an innocent act of kindness on her part. She had been so sure Adam would like to see the newly born kittens. And he had, she accepted dully. It was the thought of parting them from their mother that had distressed him...

'Cat, you were incredibly rude just now,' Kate admonished her as she came back into the kitchen. 'We have plenty of food, and I'm sure it would have been much easier for Caleb if the two of them had joined us for the meal rather than him having to go home and cook something for them both.'

Cat sat down shakily at the kitchen table. 'Believe me, I didn't mean to be rude.'

'Then why—?'

'I'm sure Cat had her reasons,' Kitty put in smoothly as she joined them in the kitchen, putting a comforting hand on Cat's shoulder.

Cat looked up at her with pained eyes. 'Did you see and hear what happened?'

Kitty squeezed her shoulder. 'I did,' she sighed. 'That poor little boy.' She bowed her head, tears glistening in her eyes. 'He's too young to be carrying pain like that around inside him.'

Kitty knew all there was to know about the pain of losing a loved one, of feeling responsible for that death. It was that same pain that had brought an abrupt end to her career twenty-five years ago, that had made her rethink the values of her life, start over, begin a new life in another country, taking her baby granddaughter with her.

Oh, the pain had obviously lessened over the years, and there had been the compensation of Kate and other members of her family. But that had only happened because Kitty was an adult, able to deal with her pain and loss on an adult level. Adam was only a child—an emotionally damaged child.

Although he wasn't going to like it any more than Cat did, she believed that Caleb was partially responsible for that damage, albeit unwittingly...

CHAPTER SEVEN

'CAT!' Toby greeted warmly, walking in the opposite direction to the one Cat was taking. 'I was just on my way to see you!'

She had already guessed that; there were no other houses the way he was going. 'To apologise, I hope?' she prompted drily.

He looked momentarily confused, and then he became shamefaced. 'I was a bit—well, I was out of line earlier,' he admitted awkwardly.

'You certainly were,' she acknowledged ruefully. 'Okay, Toby, you're forgiven,' she said, turning to continue her walk to Rose Cottage.

'Where are you going?' Toby called after her sharply, obviously having expected her to fall into step beside him on the way to Clive House.

Cat turned to look at him, auburn brows raised mockingly. 'After our earlier conversation, I don't think you really want to know!'

'Reynolds again!' he rasped harshly. 'Cat, you're running after the man, and—'

'Careful, Toby,' she warned softly, green eyes glittering. 'You're seriously in danger of stepping over that line again!'

The truth of the matter was she wasn't exactly looking forward to seeing Caleb in a few minutes. If she could have avoided it, then she most certainly would have. But she, Kate and Kitty had continued to discuss Adam over dinner, and even Kate was in agreement that something had to be

said to the little boy's father. And as Cat had already volunteered herself for the task—!

Adam was the one who had to be thought of, Kitty had
assured her. Yet the closer Cat came to Rose Cottage, all
she could think of was the coldly arrogant man who had
come to the house on Sunday afternoon…! That personality
had mainly evaporated over the last few days, as they'd
come to know Caleb a little better, but still Cat had a feeling it could return with a vengeance very shortly!

'I don't understand you, Cat.' Toby gave an angry shake
of his head. 'I've been here almost a year now, and during
all of that time I haven't seen you in the least interested in
any man; Reynolds only arrived here at the weekend, and
you know nothing about the man, and yet you can't seem
to stay away from him!'

What Toby meant by this last remark was that she hadn't
shown any interest in *him*! There was a simple reason for
that. Toby, for all his flirtation and suggestive remarks, just
didn't appeal to her in that way.

The fact that the two of them had become friends did
not give him the right to jump to conclusions—and throw
out wild accusations—where Caleb Reynolds was concerned!

'You just went over the line, Toby,' she told him coldly.
'In fact, I would advise you to keep your opinions—where
I'm concerned—to yourself in future!'

He blinked dazedly at her coldness; it was obviously not
a side of her he had ever seen before.

But then, he had never intruded in her personal life before in the way that he was now. They had become friends,
the four of them, Kate, Kitty, Toby and herself, and while
she understood that some people could become possessive
over friendships—and Toby was giving every impression
at the moment of being one of those intense people—Cat
would never allow her friendship to be owned. By anyone.

'I couldn't agree more.' She kept the smile on her face, again more for Lilley Stewart's benefit than Toby's; if it looked as if she and Toby were arguing the day after she'd had dinner with Caleb, conclusions would be jumped to that were not only wrong, but could also prove embarrassing! 'Although I'm not sure, Toby, exactly what "this" is?' she continued silkily, her eyes narrowed now.

'We're friends, Cat—'

'We certainly are,' she agreed. 'But friendship between two people does not give them the right to pass judgement on any other friendships either of them might have! In fact, I don't remember even mentioning it to you when you were seen disappearing out of the village in a car with a mysterious blonde!'

Cat had received that information compliments of Lilley—whether she wanted to know or not! In fact, she was still amazed, even after years of living here, that Lilley could manage to run the post office and keep tabs on everyone and everything that went on in the village. There had to be an art to it. Thank goodness it was one Cat had never acquired!

'What mysterious blonde?' Toby was instantly on the defensive.

'I have no idea, Toby,' Cat replied with a laugh. 'That's exactly the point I'm trying to make; I don't know, and I'm not interested in knowing!'

'Cat—'

'Toby,' she returned warningly. 'I think you've drawn quite enough attention to us for one day.' She looked pointedly towards the shop behind them. 'In any case, from what Kate said, the three of you had an enjoyable evening together, in spite of my absence.'

'That isn't the point—'

'There is no point to this conversation, Toby,' she assured him hardly. 'Now, if you wouldn't mind, I have some

'I'm only thinking of you, Cat.' He reached out and placed a placating hand on her arm. 'After all, you have a reputation to uphold in the community. And—' He broke off, frowning, as Cat laughed in soft rebuke. 'I'm not trying to be funny, Cat—'

'That's just as well—because you aren't succeeding!' she told him crisply. 'I didn't notice you being so concerned about my reputation where you're concerned? A disreputable artist—from London of all places!—''and never out of the house''.' She did a passable impression of Lilley, shaking her head at Toby as he looked affronted by the description. 'Recognise yourself, Toby?' she taunted.

He swallowed hard. 'Does she—? Has she really said that about us—?'

'About you, Toby,' Cat corrected him. 'That, and more. I learnt long ago what both truth and rumour could do to people,' she told him dully. 'The fact that most people don't give a damn which it is! So, yes, Toby, I'm going to see Caleb. Again. And no doubt five minutes after I go in the door it will be round the village that I'm involved with both of you.' She shrugged. 'The fact that it isn't true of either of you won't be believed whether I deny or ignore it!'

'And isn't it?' He pounced. 'True of either of us?' he explained at her puzzled look.

She gave a sad shake of her head. 'The answer to that, quite frankly, Toby, is no! I'm twenty-five, Toby,' she continued, 'and I haven't lived in a convent for all those years! I learnt long ago just how fickle and—and untrustworthy men can be, and I have no intention of being hurt ever again!' The pain and humiliation she had suffered at Graham Barton's unscrupulous hands was something she'd tried very hard not to think about, but that didn't mean it hadn't coloured all her future relationships with men.

'But—'

'No buts, Toby. Now, if you will excuse me?' She gave an obvious glance at her watch, the time two minutes to nine o'clock. 'I'm going to be late.'

Toby gave her a suspicious look, not in the least impressed with the way he felt he had been fobbed off. 'I think I'll go on up to the house anyway,' he said slowly.

'You do that.' Now it was Cat's turn to pat his arm placatingly. 'I'm sure Kate and Kitty will be pleased to see you.'

He looked exasperated at her bantering tone. 'One day, Cat,' he said, 'you're going to meet your match—and God help him!'

She laughed along with him at his remark, but inside she vowed fiercely, Never in your lifetime, buster, never in your lifetime!

Or in Caleb Reynolds', either, she decided a few minutes later when he opened the cottage door to her with the greeting, 'You're two minutes late!'

Not a very good beginning to what she already knew was going to be a delicate conversation. Especially as delicacy wasn't exactly her forte!

'Is Adam asleep?' she queried as she followed Caleb through to the kitchen, aware of how ruggedly male he looked in his denims and black shirt.

'An hour ago,' he replied tersely. 'Coffee or wine?' he offered.

Definitely not a good beginning. Much as she would have liked a glass of wine to see her through the conversation ahead, another part of her warned her she was going to need all her wits about her when she spoke to Caleb.

'Coffee will be fine, thank you,' she accepted, although she noticed there was no offer of a seat to go with it. 'I hope you didn't think I was being rude earlier?' She looked across at him tensely as he began to prepare the coffee.

He barely glanced at her. 'I'm quickly learning that

you're a law unto yourself, Cat. You've obviously decided we need to discuss something, so here we both are.'

'I was actually referring to the way I cut in earlier on Kate's invitation for you to join us for dinner...'

Dark brows rose over cool grey eyes. 'I wasn't aware that you did,' he said.

'Then why—? Caleb, I don't particularly want to be here, intruding on your privacy,' she burst out in a rush. 'I told you, something happened earlier. With Adam.'

He nodded, leaning back against one of the kitchen units, the smell of filtering coffee pervading the room. 'When you visited the kittens.'

'He told you?' she prompted eagerly.

'No—you did,' he came back tautly. 'Adam doesn't talk, remember?' he added hardly.

'Caleb—'

'I'm sorry, Cat. You're right, something did happen earlier; Adam has been very—difficult, since we got back to the cottage. In fact, I'm not convinced he's actually asleep.' He grimaced. 'He looked as if he was faking it to me.'

'Oh.' Cat also pulled a face, keeping her voice low. 'I don't think Adam likes me very much at the moment.' She softly explained the reason she was talking so quietly. 'He thinks I'm going to let him down,' she said sadly.

'And are you?' Caleb rasped. 'Adam has become very fond of you over the last few days; until this evening I actually thought we might be making some progress with him.' He paused briefly. 'But tonight Adam's been—uncooperative, bad-tempered, and very angry. Until just now I wasn't sure who that anger was directed at.' He looked at her, his gaze steady. 'What the hell happened earlier, Cat?'

Exactly what did you do to my son? his tone implied!

Of course, she had known it would be like this; Caleb

was always on the defensive ·when it came to his son's welfare.

'Let's just calm this all down, Caleb,' she suggested soothingly. 'Just point me in the direction of the cups, I'll pour us some coffee, and then we can sit down and talk about this quietly and calmly.'

His movements were deliberately controlled as he took down two china mugs from a cupboard. 'Black, no sugar for me, thank you,' he bit out harshly. 'And I would advise you to get to "this" very quickly, Cat,' he added frostily. 'I'm not known for my patience.'

She could believe that!

She poured their coffee, sitting down as she put the mugs down on the pine kitchen table, the cottage too small to have its own dining-room. 'Caleb,' she began hesitantly as he sat down opposite her at the table, 'when I was little— just a baby, I've since been told,' she recalled, 'my cousin came to live with us in Ireland—'

'Cat—'

'At least hear me out, Caleb,' she pleaded as he cut in, waiting until he gave a terse nod of agreement before she continued. 'My little cousin, a baby girl just a few months younger than me, was very beautiful. She looked like the angel we had put on top of the Christmas tree: baby blonde curls, an angelic face. Everyone loved her. Except me, apparently,' she admitted guiltily. 'I wasn't very nice to her, would take her toys away from her and hide them, pull the golden curls when I thought no one was looking—'

'It was a natural reaction, Cat,' Caleb dismissed. 'Until your cousin arrived, you had obviously been the baby, loved and cosseted—'

'But I still was,' she acknowledged forcefully. 'My parents had been married almost ten years when I was born; I was like a little miracle to them! In my childish mind I couldn't believe that my mummy and daddy loved me now they had this new baby, thought they must love her instead. What I'm trying to say—and not very well,' she confessed as he gave her a scathing glance, 'is that children don't have the ability to discern all the different facets and depths of love. What I need to know, so that we stand some chance of helping Adam—and I'm pretty sure you aren't going to like this—'

'I would do anything to help Adam, Cat,' Caleb ground out fiercely. 'Anything!' He glared across the width of the table at her.

As she had known would happen, the man from Sunday afternoon was back in full force…!

'This isn't something physical for you actually to do, Caleb,' Cat told him carefully. 'This is something for you to talk about. The way I behaved with my baby cousin is, in adult life, something I'm deeply ashamed of, something I actually prefer not to talk about.'

'You were a child,' Caleb came back. 'You didn't understand.'

'Adam is also a child,' she put in slowly. 'And he doesn't understand, either.' She drew in a ragged breath. 'I believe—and I admit I could be wrong,' she acknowledged as he looked at her again sceptically, 'that something happened on the day of the accident, something Adam prefers not to talk about. And I—I think it has some sort of connection with being taken away from his mother!'

She inwardly cringed after making this last bold statement, knowing by the way Caleb's expression darkened that she had been right to assume he would resent—deeply!—her intrusion into what he considered private family business. But if she didn't talk to him about it, who would? Certainly not Adam…

'I told you you wouldn't like what I was going to say,' she finished.

He shut his eyes momentarily, then opened them. 'It isn't

so much what you're saying... That day, even before the accident, was one of the bleakest of my life.'

'Adam's too, I think,' Cat nodded. 'But he doesn't have the adult logic to alleviate whatever it is he's feeling. Caleb, today, when I showed Adam the kittens, in view of what you told me yesterday, I—I said he would perhaps be able to choose one of the kittens for himself once they were old enough to leave their mother.' She swallowed hard. 'I've never seen such raw pain in a child of three! He looked horrified at the suggestion the kittens would be taken from their mother, and then he ran off back to the kitchen—that's the reason I returned a few minutes after he did.'

Caleb stood up forcefully, totally dominating the small confines of the kitchen area, his head almost touching the low-beamed ceiling. 'God damn it, he couldn't have— He was upstairs—' His jaw set in fierce denial. 'As you've probably guessed,' he bit out accusingly, 'Alicia, Adam's mother, was leaving me on the day of the accident!'

Cat hadn't guessed any such thing! If she had thought about it at all, she had been going along the lines of an argument with his wife, something to do with taking Adam out with her that day, and Caleb not wanting her to do so, or, alternatively, that Caleb should have been with them that day, and for some reason had been unable to be, and that perhaps the couple had argued over that. She certainly hadn't thought it was quite as devastating as Caleb's wife actually leaving him...!

Cat's immediate thought following this was that Alicia must either have been a very brave woman—or a very stupid one!

Caleb Reynolds, for all that he possessed a cloak of civilisation, was nonetheless as fiercely savage under that thin veneer of sophistication as his ancient ancestors had been— and what he considered was his would belong to him body and soul!

So which had Alicia Reynolds been—brave or stupid? And why had she been leaving Caleb? To be loved and cherished by this man would surely be—

No! She didn't want to be loved and cherished by any man, least of all one as arrogant and self-assured as Caleb! She was doing all this for Adam, had no personal interest in this whatsoever. It didn't matter to her that his wife—

It did matter to her!

Cat looked up at him with widely startled eyes now. He was dominating, arrogant, mocking; she couldn't possibly fall in love with such a man. But he was also warm and funny, another inner voice counter-argued. He loved his son with a fierce tenderness that was endearing.

But exactly how fierce had that love been for Adam six months ago…?

She swallowed hard. 'I see,' she murmured huskily, doing nothing of the sort.

Caleb looked across at her, his mouth twisting scathingly. 'I doubt it,' he rasped. 'Alicia was a student of mine eight years ago, tiny, delicate, with a fiercely enquiring mind. But she was also ambitious, determined to succeed in her chosen field, and nothing came of our friendship. We didn't meet again for almost three years after she left my tutorship, by which time she—'

'I don't think I need to hear all this,' Cat cut in awkwardly, uncomfortable at hearing how he had met and fallen in love with his wife. She really didn't want to know how tiny and delicate his wife had been, or how intelligent!

Caleb looked at her steadily. 'Oh, I think you do, Cat,' he finally said quietly. 'We fell in love. But unfortunately,' he went on hardly, 'we fell in love with different things. I can see your confusion.' He sat down again wearily. 'Alicia's love for me was— You may never have heard of Caleb Reynolds, Cat, but in the world of archaeology I'm quite well known!'

'I realise that,' she accepted. And she did realise it, had read his two books this last week, had ordered others of his from a bookshop in town, and she was fully aware now of just how important he was in his chosen field.

But she really didn't want to hear about this match made in heaven. Although it couldn't have been that heavenly if Alicia had been leaving him...? But death, the finality of it, often had a way of dulling any faults, leaving only memories of the good times. In some cases that could be a blessing, in others it could be soul-destroying...

'Alicia admired me,' Caleb continued harshly. 'Respected me. Knew that as my wife— It wasn't me, the man, she loved!' he rasped. 'What she loved was my reputation in architecture.' He gave a hard, derisive laugh. 'I seriously believe that the fact I was also a man came as something of a shock to her!' He paused momentarily and then continued. 'She hadn't expected— She wasn't marrying me, the *man*, a man with all the normal feelings and desires!'

Cat could only stare at him in disbelief; anyone more male, more virilely male, she had yet to meet. It was something she had been aware of where Caleb was concerned from their very first meeting. It was also something she hadn't been unaware of for even a moment since!

He gave a heavy sigh. 'Alicia fell in love with my reputation, and I fell in love with the way she looked, and the fact that we had our careers in common—none of which is a basis for a lifelong marriage! Alicia hated the physical side of marriage,' he said flatly. 'She said it was undignified, could see nothing beautiful or loving about it.'

Not because this man hadn't been a loving or experienced lover, Cat felt sure. In fact, she knew he was. Alicia Reynolds had been a stupid woman, after all!

And Caleb—how had he coped with his wife finding the physical side of their marriage repulsive? By being cold, and arrogant, with a shield around his heart...?

'Luckily for both of us, that part of our marriage came to an abrupt end shortly after our honeymoon, when Alicia found she was pregnant. Yes, I did say end, Cat,' he confirmed at her start of surprise. 'I had no desire to make love to a woman who was repulsed by the act, and Alicia just had no desire at all! But there were compensations, one of them being Adam; we both loved him from the day he was born.' His expression lightened at the thought of his son. 'I think we reached an uneasy truce that day, which was to become the basis of our marriage for the next three years.' He gave a bark of a laugh. 'We made a good job of it too, because to all intents and purposes we were a happy family.'

Cat couldn't imagine living in the way he described, couldn't understand how he had tolerated a marriage that was as cold as his had been. Although she could see that Adam would be a great incentive to leave things as they were.

But something had obviously happened to change that...?

'Six months ago Alicia decided she was going back to work.' Caleb seemed to read some of her thoughts. 'She accepted a job as assistant on a dig in Egypt. It was for a year. And in the circumstances she felt it would be a perfect opportunity for us to finally part, and eventually divorce. She also informed me that she intended taking Adam with her,' he concluded, eyes narrowed to chilly slits.

'Ah,' Cat breathed softly, realising as she did so that she had been holding her breath as he talked. Because she simply couldn't believe what he was telling her. That he had tolerated such a sterile marriage. But at the same time she knew that every word he was saying was true. Alicia, Cat felt, had married Caleb believing it would further her career to be married to such a prominent architectural historian, but the reality of marriage was something she'd been unprepared for, something she'd refused to participate in. Which had left Caleb married to a woman who neither loved him nor wanted him.

Really, in the circumstances he had been left with, what choice had he had? Separation, and with it the loss of his baby? To have made love with his wife, knowing how she felt about it, would have been unacceptable to a man like Caleb.

Just as, three years later, it had been unacceptable to him that Alicia walk away from the marriage with his son...

'You argued the day of the accident about who would keep Adam,' Cat guessed. 'Is it possible Adam could have overheard that argument?' She frowned across at Caleb.

'It's possible, yes,' he answered distractedly. 'But why would that have caused such a trauma in him, he won't talk? All he could have heard was how much we both loved and wanted him.' He shook his head in confusion.

Cat had come to that realisation as this conversation had unfurled, and she had come up with an answer, of sorts. 'What if—?' She drew in a deep breath; she had come this far, she had to go on! 'This is pure guesswork on my part,' she admitted. 'But what if Adam, having heard the two of you arguing, and then being driven off by his mother, believed that he would never see you again? In those circumstances, I believe the child would cry for the lost parent...' She hesitated. 'And if that's what was happening when the accident occurred, wouldn't he now be consumed with guilt, because his mummy died?'

Caleb looked at her dazedly. 'Do you really think that's what happened that day?'

'I told you, I'm only guessing, but after his reaction earlier to the kittens being taken from their mother... It's only natural for a child to have cried for the parent he believed he was leaving behind. Look at it from his point of view;

the two of you had argued about who would keep him, and then after the argument his mother drove off with him—'

'She was only going shopping,' Caleb protested. 'We were going to—discuss the situation again later that evening.'

'But Adam didn't know that!' Cat reasoned. 'He probably thought he was leaving you for ever. He was just a baby, Caleb, being taken from the father he obviously adores; of course he would have cried for you. And maybe, just maybe, that could have distracted Alicia from concentrating on her driving properly; God knows, a child crying can be distressing at any time, let alone when you're driving!'

'Oh, God...!' Caleb stood up to pace the small confines of the kitchen. 'I never thought— I didn't realise—'

'But how could you have done, Caleb? You had just lost your wife, Adam his mother; the last six months have been difficult enough, I'm sure, without apportioning blame.' Although she was sure he had done that where his own actions were concerned! 'Or dealing with feelings of guilt that shouldn't be there.' She went back to Adam. 'And you still have to bear in mind that all this is only conjecture on my part. I could be wrong.'

'But it fits, damn it,' Caleb muttered savagely. 'Only too well!' he accepted grimly.

As he said, it did fit, but that still didn't mean it was right. 'Go carefully, Caleb,' she warned worriedly. 'If I'm wrong, and you talk to Adam about this, it could just make the situation ten times worse!'

But Caleb no longer seemed to be listening to her, lost in his own inner turmoil. Which, in the circumstances, was understandable. Because of the things she had asked and said, Caleb had had to relive a very painful time in his life.

Cat could easily understand, with their shared interest, how Caleb and Alicia had formed a relationship, but she still couldn't understand how the other woman could have fallen in love with his reputation and name, and not have loved the man, the physical man, as well. God, she was so aware of him on that level herself, the whole idea was simply unacceptable!

'So what do you think of me now, little Cat?' He suddenly turned on her viciously. 'A man who couldn't even keep his own wife in his bed!'

'Caleb, don't!' She groaned at his self-deprecation. 'Some women are like that, it doesn't mean—'

'Doesn't mean what, Cat?' he cut in tauntingly, pulling her roughly to her feet. 'That I'm not attractive to women? Or that I'm not a good lover?' His face was only inches away from hers now.

She shook her head, wincing at the grasp of his fingers on her arms. 'You know I don't think either of those things, Caleb—'

'Do I?' he ground out, his eyes glittering deeply grey, nothing like the teasing man she had spent the previous evening with, the man who was caring enough to want her to telephone him as soon as she got in, just so that he knew she was safely home! 'I don't have a clue what you think, Cat; I never have. But I know what I think,' he breathed as he released her arms and pulled her closer to him, his mouth coming down on hers.

Cat was prepared for the strength of his kiss, had half been expecting it since he had talked of his wife and their sterile marriage. And because she had been expecting it she didn't pull away, her arms moving about his waist as she returned his kiss, not with the same demand, but with a desire that certainly matched his own.

In spite of herself, she was falling in love with this man, and so his pain became her own, exploding into a passion that made their kisses fevered, Cat's lips against the pulsing column of his throat now, her body arched into the demanding hardness of his.

One of her hands became entangled in the darkness of the hair at his nape, her breath catching in her throat as he moved down and the moist heat of his mouth closed over her turgid nipple, the thin material of her tee shirt his only barrier; as she felt the caress of his tongue over that fiery tip, it was no barrier at all!

Her neck was arched back further, her breath coming in rasped gasps as burning pleasure coursed through her body, wanting more—oh, so much more! She wanted Caleb. All of him. The virile strength of him. She wanted this man completely—

'No!'

Caleb thrust her away from him so suddenly, she staggered and almost fell, grasping onto the kitchen table, her legs feeling weak without his arms to support her, her mouth swollen from his kisses, her cheeks flushed, her eyes brightly green and feverish as she stared across at him confusedly. He had wanted her too, she knew he had, so why—?

'Go, Cat,' he gritted before turning away from her, the darkness of his hair tousled from her caressing fingers, making it look more ruffled himself as he ran agitated fingers through it. 'Go, Cat,' he repeated forcefully. 'Before I do something we're both going to regret!'

Would she regret it? Probably. Later. Much later. But at this moment she still wanted him, still felt the desire pulsing—

He turned quickly as she made no move to leave, grey eyes cold now, his face taut with anger. 'You won't be doing me any favours, Cat,' he bit out scathingly, his gaze raking over her contemptuously. 'I have no need to prove I'm still a man! There were women before Alicia, and there could have been plenty since her. Only since the disaster of my marriage I'm just a little more choosy who I—'

'Stop it!' She put her hands over her ears, tears in her eyes, not wanting to hear about other women he had made love with. 'I'm going,' she choked. 'There's no need for you to be cruel!'

'Oh, Cat!' he groaned, reaching out a hand towards her.

She flinched away from him. 'Don't!' she told him sharply. 'As someone pointed out to me earlier this evening, I don't even know you! And after this evening I don't think I want to either!' She turned and almost ran from the kitchen, and the cottage, keeping her movements to a hurried walk once she was outside, so as not to draw attention to herself, but desperately needing to get away from the scene of her humiliation.

She had come here this evening with the intention of helping Adam. But all she had succeeded in doing was hurting herself.

She should have known, should have remembered just how selfish and single-minded men could be. Graham had tried to use her, and now Caleb had— He had humiliated her almost as much as Graham had, but in a different way.

She never wanted to see Caleb Reynolds again!

CHAPTER EIGHT

'THAT was Caleb,' Kate told Cat as she came back from answering the telephone the next evening. 'He apologised for Adam not being at playschool today. He also said Adam won't be in tomorrow, either,' she added.

He hadn't asked to talk to her, Cat realised miserably. And why should he, after the way they had parted last night? He would no more wish to see or speak to her than she did him!

And yet...

Part of her wanted to see Caleb again. The part of her that was falling in love with him.

But she had made a fool of herself; more to the point, Caleb had let her make a fool of herself! She was glad she didn't have to see him again for the rest of the week. Maybe by Monday her pride would be firmly back in place!

Because it had certainly taken a beating yesterday. She had been dreading seeing Caleb again this morning when he brought Adam in. But as the morning had passed, and there was no sign of either of them, that dread had turned to concern. For Adam, she told herself firmly. If he had happened to overhear anything the evening before...!

'Did he say why?' Cat prompted as casually as she was able, although she knew Kate must be aware that wasn't the way she was feeling inside. The manner in which Cat had burst into the house yesterday evening, her humiliation having turned to anger as she walked home, must have told her friend that!

Although, to give Kate her due, she hadn't pried, either last night or today. However, her curiosity, especially after

Adam's non-appearance today, must be brimming over. But it had never been Kate's approach to force an issue; she would simply sit and wait until Cat felt ready to talk about it.

As she no doubt would, once her anger at herself had abated a little. The anger she felt towards Caleb, for being the cause of her own churning emotions, would take a lot longer to rationalise and accept!

Kate rejoined Cat at the kitchen table as they shelled the fresh peas for dinner. 'Family commitments, was all he said.'

Very helpful! Caleb had mentioned having a sister, and a little niece of two, and yet somehow Cat didn't think that was the 'family commitment'...

'I hope everything is all right with Adam,' she said worriedly.

Kate touched her arm reassuringly. 'Caleb is a very loving father, Cat, and from what you've said about your conversation with him last night I'm sure he will handle the situation, and Adam, tactfully.'

From what little she had hissed when she'd got in...! Because she hadn't told Kate or Kitty anything that Caleb had said about his marriage, only that there had been an argument between husband and wife on the day of the accident. And she had no intention—ever!—of telling either of them what had happened between Caleb and herself at the end of that conversation!

She was still confused as to why she should feel so drawn to Caleb. She had never been this attracted to any man before, knew there would have been no protest from her if Caleb had wanted to make love to her yesterday evening. In fact, it was his rejection of her that had sparked off the row between them that had made her leave so hurriedly.

Typical. She never did anything the way other people

did. But her father claimed she had been contrary from the day she was born, so she probably wasn't going to change now...

Sometimes she missed her parents, and Ireland, so much, it was like a physical pain. Her father, short, with red hair and green eyes, like Cat herself, would have made light of last night with a few teasing words about the English. It wouldn't have taken away her pain, or lessened her feelings towards Caleb, but her father would certainly have helped her to put things into perspective.

Maybe she should think about going home for the weekend soon; she certainly needed to be able to put something into perspective!

'Toby called in after you went out yesterday evening.' Kate changed the subject.

'Toby is a pain!' Cat came back without hesitation, that conversation still rankling too.

Kate grimaced. 'He was doing his brotherly bit. But Kitty told him he had no reason to be in the least concerned about you, because you were in completely trustworthy company!'

Caleb might be trustworthy; it was herself she didn't trust!

She raised her brows. 'Kitty told him that?'

'She certainly did,' Kate confirmed. 'Your Mr Reynolds seems to have made a good impression on her.'

'He isn't *my* Mr Anything,' Cat snapped. 'And as to the other, I have no idea how— Kitty has never even met him!'

'Ah, but I've seen him, my dear,' Kitty told her as she came through to join them, looking much younger than her seventy-two years, in a blue sundress, her blonde hair loose about her shoulders. 'I was always a good judge of men.'

Cat wondered just how good a judge of men Kitty would think herself if she were to tell her how yesterday evening had ended. Although she accepted that after their conver-

sation emotions had been running high, her response to
Caleb was something she still felt surprised about. But that
was still no reason for Caleb to have been quite so cruel at
the end!

'You should invite him here for dinner one evening, Cat,'
Kitty told her as she began to lay the table in preparation
for their meal. 'Kate tells me it was an ancestor of his that
actually built this house.'

'Yes,' Cat confirmed flatly. 'But what happens if he
comes here for dinner and recognises you?' she reasoned,
every part of her screaming in protest at the idea of Caleb
coming for a meal. If she'd had to meet him this morning
when he brought Adam to playschool that would have been
bad enough, but, the way she felt towards him at the moment, there was no way she could be polite to him!

'Mr Reynolds doesn't appear to me to be the sort of
person who likes his privacy invaded, let alone wish to pry
into other people's,' Kitty said slowly. 'Besides, as I told
you two girls long ago, just because I've opted out, so to
speak, I do not want it affecting either of your lives.'

'Girls!' Cat repeated with a derisive shake of her head.
'We're neither of us that any more, Kitty.'

'Exactly,' she came back. 'It's well past time you both
found some gorgeous man to settle down with and had
children of your own!'

'You're starting to sound like Toby now,' Cat said disgustedly.

'He'd be the gorgeous man, of course,' Kate added sa-
tirically.

'Of course,' Kitty acknowledged with a smile.

But as first Friday, and then the weekend, passed, they saw
neither Toby nor Caleb. The latter Cat was frankly relieved
about, although she couldn't stop herself gazing down at
Rose Cottage once she went to bed, just to check if there

were any lights on. The fact that there weren't told her that Caleb's family commitment had take him out of the area.

But it was most unusual for four days to pass without Toby putting in an appearance. By Sunday evening Cat thought that perhaps one of them should go down to Toby's cottage to check on him. After all, he could be ill, and there was no one else in the village he was particularly friendly with. There was always the possibility he was staying away because he believed Cat was still angry with him...

Kitty had already decided she was going to do some gardening in the cool of the evening, and Kate said she had a headache and intended lying down for a while until it went away, which left Cat with the task of going down to Toby's cottage. Not that she particularly minded; after the last four days of tension, she was in danger of getting a headache herself if she didn't get out of the house for a while!

Toby's cottage was at the other end of the village, and the walk would help clear her head. She even had a chance to give a brief glance at Rose Cottage on her way past! No car in the driveway, no lights on inside; Caleb was still away...

Toby's cottage seemed just as deserted when she arrived ten minutes later, no lights on at the front—although that was nothing to go on; Toby could be in the back room. But there was no rakish MG sports car in the driveway either...

So much for finding a gorgeous man and settling down with him; she and Kate seemed to have frightened away the only two available ones in the area!

Nonetheless, Cat went up to the door and rang the bell, aware that Toby could be working at the back of the cottage in the long room that had been built on by the last owner, the man had been a train fanatic, and had set up his own 'line' in this room; now Toby had transformed it into a studio for himself. The fact that Toby's car wasn't in the driveway was also no real indication that he wasn't at home either; the car was twenty years old, with a tendency to break down, so Toby could just have abandoned it and walked home!

No, lack of lights or car was no indication that Toby wasn't here, and Cat walked around the back of the cottage to where the studio was located. This long brick structure wasn't visible from the front of the cottage, and didn't really fit in with the rest of the picturesque building, which was probably one of the reasons it hadn't sold when put on the market a couple of years ago, and the absent owner had finally decided to rent it out instead. But it was perfect for Toby's studio, he had once assured her enthusiastically.

But all the doors were locked at the back of the cottage too, even the one to the studio, a quick glance inside here showing her all Toby's works turned to lean against the wall, the painting he was working on at the moment shrouded in a sheet. With another showing in a London gallery due in just three months, Cat knew that he was working hard to get ready for it.

But he wasn't working today, Cat realised with disappointment, starting to walk away. Strange. Toby could be extremely irritating at times—especially when he tried to interfere in her private life!—but she had felt his absence the last four days.

Almost as much as she had missed Caleb, came the betraying thought...

She didn't miss Caleb! He meant nothing to her. Nothing!

She had told herself this several times over the last few days, in an effort to convince herself she was not falling in love with him, and yet the ache she felt inside whenever she thought of him seemed to make a liar out of her. He was—

'Like a lift home?'

Here!

Her breath caught in her throat, and her heart began to pound erratically, just at the sound of his voice. She didn't need to turn to recognise the driver of the car parked at the pavement beside her.

She hadn't seen him since— She wasn't sure she could face him again after— She had behaved—

'Get in the car, Cat,' he ordered arrogantly. 'I'm offering to drive you home, not ravish you!'

She turned at the scorn in his voice, two spots of angry colour in her cheeks, her eyes flashing—only to find him grinning widely at her.

'I thought that might get a reaction,' he drawled, leaning over to open the passenger door for her to get in.

'Am I that predictable?' she muttered as she climbed in the car beside him, a quick glance in the back revealing a sleeping Adam. She might be none too happy about accepting this lift from Caleb, but she didn't want Adam to wake up to the sound of the two of them arguing!

'Unfortunately not,' Caleb answered grimly before glancing over at the cottage she had obviously just come from. 'Been visiting friends?'

Cat met his gaze unflinchingly. 'He wasn't at home,' she bit out tersely.

'He?' Caleb repeated softly, eyes narrowed to steely slits. 'Westward?' he guessed harshly as he accelerated the car rapidly away.

Cat clutched at the seat belt she had been in the process of fastening, barely managing to click it into place as she was forced back against the seat by the speed of the car. 'Yes,' she answered through gritted teeth.

'And do you often pay calls on him at his cottage?'

'Is that any of your business?' she returned caustically, glancing back at Adam again to make sure he was still sleeping.

Caleb shrugged. 'As a parent—'

'Oh, please, Caleb,' Cat cut in exasperatedly, 'give me a break! Parent or not, my private life is exactly that— private.' She seemed to have had this conversation before, and quite recently too!

It was amazing, really. She had lived quietly for years, quite happy with her life, but over the last week it had been thrown into chaos. Since Caleb's arrival!

'I didn't hear you making the same objection when I called at your cottage on Wednesday evening!' Not from him, anyway!

Caleb shot her a sidelong glance. 'I wasn't behaving as a parent, then,' he returned mockingly.

Cat gave him a scathing look. 'How nice to be able to pick and choose what you want to be! I'm me all the time,' she added tersely.

He nodded. 'Prickly, outspoken, impulsive, beautiful to look at—'

'You—'

'—and totally refreshing to be around,' he continued as if she hadn't spoken. 'That's a pretty lethal combination in one woman!'

Cat looked across at him, expecting to find sarcasm in his expression, and instead finding only rueful self-derision.

She made no reply. What could she say to a remark like that? Especially as she had decided during the last four days that the best thing she could do where this man was concerned was to keep some distance between them. He had problems of his own he had to deal with, and she could certainly do without the complication of him in her life.

Caleb chuckled wryly. 'So there is another way of silencing that outspoken tongue of yours!' he said quietly, with amusement.

Cat's mouth set stubbornly as she laced her fingers together in her lap—the latter so that she wouldn't do anything 'impulsive'!—knowing exactly what other way he knew of silencing her. And the less said about that the better!

To her relief she saw they were approaching the house. She wasn't sure how much longer she could have remained silent—because she was very tempted to tell Caleb exactly what she thought of him—and his damned mockery. Because there was no way she could look on this man's brand of flattery as anything else!

Unfortunately, however, as Caleb stopped the car beside the gateway, Cat could see Kitty still in the garden, taking the dead flowers off some of the rose bushes!

It was an encounter Cat had wanted—hoped!—to avoid. Especially after what Kitty had said earlier about inviting Caleb to dinner one evening. But as she saw Kitty rise to her feet, putting up a hand in greeting as she walked over to the gate, Cat knew her hope had been in vain!

CHAPTER NINE

CAT scrambled quickly out of the car, even though she knew her haste would be in vain, but Caleb climbed out from behind the wheel much more slowly to stroll over and join the two women as they stood at the gate, grey eyes narrowed on the smiling Kitty.

Cat tried to look at her through Caleb's eyes, seeing the tall, elegant woman, her upright stature and bearing belying her years, blonde hair loose about her shoulders, her figure a little too curvaceous to be called slender, her face bearing few lines, blue eyes glowing with warmth.

But what Cat was really looking for was a resemblance to the operatic star Katherine Maitland—it was all too easy to see that this was exactly who Kitty was!

'Mr Reynolds,' Kitty greeted warmly, holding out her hand, and then laughed self-consciously as she became aware of the dirt on it from the gardening. 'Gardening can be such a messy business.' She shook Caleb's hand with a hastily wiped one of her own. 'But I do so love to get my hands in the soil, don't you, Mr—?'

'Please call me Caleb,' he put in smoothly. 'And I'm sorry to have to admit I'm not a gardener—Kitty.'

'Oh, but you really should try it, Caleb,' Kitty advised enthusiastically. 'I find it very therapeutic.'

'I think I may have to give it a try while I'm at Rose Cottage,' he accepted ruefully.

It wasn't exactly a role Cat could picture Caleb in, down on his hands and knees tending the fertile ground!

'You'll love it,' Kitty assured him laughingly. 'Do you

have time to come in for a coffee, Caleb?' she offered brightly.

'Unfortunately Adam is asleep.' He glanced back to the car. 'He's had a very boisterous weekend with his young cousin,' he explained affectionately. 'He's worn himself out. So I'm afraid I'll have to take a rain-check on the coffee, thank you, Kitty.'

Cat breathed a sigh of relief at his refusal. In fact, she hadn't been able to look at Caleb at all since he got out of the car; she didn't dare; she was frightened of what she might see in his face! Because of the way the conversation had gone, she had been spared making a formal introduction between the two, but Caleb was far from stupid, and, more importantly, he was a Katherine Maitland fan!

'Come to dinner instead, Caleb,' Kitty invited warmly. 'Adam too, of course,' she smiled.

Cat had known this invitation was coming, of course, but even so she wished Kitty hadn't made it. A whole evening sitting there on tenterhooks, knowing what had passed between them, and waiting for Caleb to say he knew exactly who Kitty was, would be intolerable!

'If it's to be an evening, I would prefer to leave Adam at the cottage with a babysitter,' Caleb said firmly. 'He's still very young, and too many late nights tend to make him—fractious.'

'Whatever suits you best,' Kitty accepted pleasantly. 'You have a very adorable son, Caleb.'

His brows rose. 'Cat mentioned the two of you had met.'

'Several days ago,' Kitty nodded. 'Adam was playing in the garden with Cat,' she explained as he still looked puzzled. 'I believe you were in the house talking to Kate.'

'That's right,' he said slowly, eyeing Kitty speculatively, obviously wondering how much she knew about his son.

Kitty met that probing gaze unflinchingly. 'You must be

very proud of him.' She squeezed Caleb's arm understandingly.

'I am,' he acknowledged huskily, the two of them tacitly acknowledging the accident six months ago, and Adam's reaction to it.

'Kate was telling me that it was your ancestor, Clive Reynolds, who actually designed and built this house.' Kitty briskly changed the subject.

'My great-great-grandfather,' he nodded.

Again Cat didn't look at him, although they both knew exactly how many 'greats' it was before grandfather!

'It really is a very small world, isn't it?' Kitty said with one of her bright smiles.

Caleb agreed. 'Much smaller than I had realised,' he murmured slowly.

Now Cat did look at him, sharply, before looking quickly away again. He knew! He hadn't come right out and said it, but he might just as well have done, that slight raising of one eyebrow as he met her gaze unflinchingly telling her that he knew exactly who Kitty was!

The name Kitty wasn't used to confuse or deceive anyone; it was the name Cat had always known her by, the older woman preferring to use the much friendlier shortening of her name; Katherine, she had stated, was reserved for the stage.

And this man remembered, Cat was sure, seeing Kitty performing on one!

'Dinner tomorrow evening, then, Caleb,' Kitty told him. 'Subject to your getting a babysitter.'

'I would like that,' he agreed. 'Subject to the babysitter.'

Cat couldn't see there being too much of a problem with that; she doubted Jane had too much else to do on a Monday evening. No, the problem with Caleb coming to dinner tomorrow evening had nothing to do with his babysitting arrangements, and everything to do with spending at least three hours in his company, not to mention waiting for him to say something about Katherine Maitland!

It was too late to do anything about it now, but she and Kate really should have been more forceful in advising Kitty not to invite Caleb to dinner. However, Kitty, because many had tried to protect her over the last twenty-five years, really had no idea of the interest her identity still had for certain people.

It wasn't much more than a year ago that some woman had been snooping around the village in search of information on Katherine Maitland. The village people, as usual, had closed ranks and told the woman, who they'd all believed was a reporter looking for a story, that Katherine Maitland hadn't lived there for years.

Kitty would be horrified if she knew about such incidents, had never been able to understand why her retirement from public life so that she might bring up her granddaughter in peace and quiet should hold such interest. But Kate and Cat knew it was the scandal that had also been attached to her retirement which still engendered interest, and they had learnt, over the years, who was not to be trusted with Kitty's identity. Toby represented no threat to Kitty's privacy, had always accepted her as just Kate's grandmother, having no idea she had ever been anything else. Caleb, however, was not as unknowledgeable...

'Lovely,' Kitty accepted happily. 'Seven-thirty for eight. Now I'll leave you and Cat to say goodnight.' She looked up at the darkening sky. 'I seem to have lost the light for gardening,' she shrugged, moving away to gather up her gardening tools before going back into the house.

The silence she left behind her was filled with a tension that Cat, for one, didn't feel inclined to break. She didn't want to have a conversation with Caleb concerning Kitty!

'Cat—'

'I had better be going in too,' she cut in hurriedly, looking at something—actually, nothing!—over his left shoulder. Because she couldn't actually look at Caleb. Not yet. Although she already knew him well enough to realise he would have plenty he wanted to say to her! He had mentioned Katherine Maitland to them on that very first meeting, and hadn't she and Kate both pleaded ignorance? Now Caleb had to realise they hadn't actually been dishonest with him, but they had definitely been evasive!

'Will Adam be coming to playschool in the morning?' she prompted lightly.

'I can't see any reason why not,' Caleb answered slowly, still frowning.

Cat moistened her lips. 'I— We thought perhaps your business in the area was finished…?' 'We' hadn't thought any such thing; in fact, she doubted Kate had given it a second thought. But then, Kate hadn't been kissed by this man until she'd lost her senses…!

'No,' he drawled. 'Hoping, Cat?' he added tauntingly.

'Not in the least,' she clipped. 'As Kitty said a few moments ago, Adam is an adorable child—'

'I don't believe we were talking about Adam, Cat,' Caleb parried.

'Well, *I* was.' Her eyes flashed deeply green in warning as she glared at him. 'I'll look forward to seeing him in the morning.'

'But not me tomorrow night, hmm?' he guessed shrewdly.

Cat looked up at him unblinkingly. 'I believe you are Kitty's guest, not mine. I happen to have other plans for tomorrow evening,' she told him stubbornly—and then wished she hadn't felt challenged into making such a claim.

Because she didn't have any other plans for tomorrow evening! And she didn't think Kitty was going to appreciate her making herself absent, either, sure that the older woman had half made the invitation in the mistaken belief that Cat was interested in Caleb!

What on earth had made her say she was going out? Because she had a feeling she might have to back-pedal on that claim before tomorrow night!

Caleb looked at her coldly now. 'Going to call on Westward again?' he challenged.

Her head went back defiantly at his tone. 'And what if I am?'

He gave her a despairing look. 'Maybe things have changed, but I always thought it was the man who did the chasing!'

Back-pedal? No, she damn well wouldn't! She couldn't imagine what had ever attracted her to this man in the first place! He was rude, arrogant—and condescending! How dared he pass judgement on her in this way? Kitty would just have to be annoyed with her tomorrow—because there was no way Cat could sit down and eat a meal with this man; she was likely to end up throwing it over his head!

'That's an extremely old-fashioned view, Caleb,' she told him with unconcealed sarcasm.

'Maybe,' he rasped. 'But it seemed to work!'

'For the man, perhaps,' she replied dismissively—having no idea why she was being so adamant; she had never chased after a man in her life. She never would. But Caleb just seemed to bring out the defensive side of her. 'Personally, I thank God the days of a woman waiting docilely for a particular man to notice her are long past!' she stated.

Caleb's mouth twisted. 'I doubt very much that you have ever waited docilely anywhere, Cat! I'm still not sure I would care to have the woman do the asking.'

She quirked auburn brows. 'You didn't seem to have a problem when Kitty did it a few minutes ago,' she reminded him.

He gave a snort. 'I very much doubt that Kitty has romantic intentions towards me!'

Cat doubted it too. She also didn't think, in the circumstances, it was exactly wise to bring Kitty back into the
conversation. The problem was, caution seemed to go out
the window—in more ways than one!—whenever she was
around this man!

'Nevertheless, I'm sure you will have an enjoyable evening,' she assured him. No matter what the opposition, she
was not going to be there! 'Now I really must get in; I have
things to do before tomorrow. And you have Adam to put
to bed,' she got in firmly as Caleb would have spoken
again.

His mouth tightened. 'So I do. But before you make
other plans for Tuesday evening too, I would like to see
you then. Perhaps we could go out to dinner somewhere?'
He watched her closely.

Cat deliberately didn't meet his assessing look—again!
The two of them go out to dinner? Alone? She didn't think
so!

'I'm sure you don't want to have a babysitter for Adam
two evenings in a row,' she commented, knowing by the
way Caleb's expression darkened that he had forgotten all
about that. 'Besides,' she went on determinedly, 'I already
have other plans for Tuesday evening too.' Even if all she
could come up with was washing her hair! She did not want
to be put in a position where she couldn't get away from
this man—or his questions!

Dark brows rose over icy grey eyes. 'Westward again?'
he demanded.

Cat tossed back her head, red curls bouncing. 'I do have
other friends!'

Caleb sighed heavily, shaking his head. 'I'm sure you
do. Cat, we seem to have got off to a bad start this evening—'

'Only this evening?' she interrupted. 'As I recall, we didn't end the evening too well last week, either!' Embarrassed colour entered her cheeks as she recalled the way she had fled his cottage. 'I think it's best that in future we just stay out of each other's way, Caleb. We just seem to annoy each other.'

'I don't think it's annoyance at all, Cat; I think we—'

'I really do have to go, Caleb.' She moved sharply away from him, sure he had been about to reach out and take her in his arms. She didn't dare let him even touch her; he would feel the way she was trembling if he did. And it wasn't through anger or fear!

There was just *something* about Caleb that made her totally aware of him in every way, but mainly on a physical level, filling her with a primitive need of him that was in contrast to everything she had just said to him. Because part of her was 'waiting'—for Caleb to make love to her! That feeling hadn't diminished in the slightest in the last four days; in fact, it had grown stronger!

'I'll see you and Adam in the morning,' she said with finality, turning and hurrying towards the house.

'Cat...?'

She froze as he called after her softly, turning slowly back to face him. 'Yes?' she prompted warily.

'You can't run away for ever, you know,' he told her huskily.

The flush in her cheeks was from anger this time. Had she somehow, in the course of their brief relationship, allowed him to see her past disillusionment with men? 'I'm not running away from anything, Caleb,' she declared. 'I'm simply walking back into my home!'

'You're being deliberately obtuse,' he ground out.

Green eyes sparkled with resentment. 'Would you prefer it if I were deliberately rude?'

'I would prefer it if you were honest!'

'Honest,' she repeated, nodding her head slowly. 'Okay, Caleb, if honesty is what you want, honesty is what you're going to get—'

'I have a feeling I'm going to regret this,' he murmured self-derisively.

'And I have a feeling you regret very little, Caleb,' she told him scathingly. 'The fact is that I just don't want to get involved—'

'Too late, Cat—we're already involved,' he cut in, eyes focused firmly on her. 'But why are you pushing me away? Who was he, Cat? What—?'

'He?' she repeated sharply—she *had* given herself away!

'The man who hurt you so badly that you shy away from other relationships,' Caleb answered quietly. 'Who was he? What did he do to you?'

Cat drew in a deep breath, forcing herself to tackle a reply. 'Stop trying to change the subject, Caleb,' she evaded. 'Just accept that we're too different—'

'You're a woman, and I'm a man,' he conceded sardonically.

'—in outlook, background, and lifestyle,' she finished, with an impatient glare at him for his levity, 'for us ever to really be friends. I—'

'I thought we already were friends.'

Cat shook her head in denial. 'Far from it!' It was relaxing to be around friends, comfortable, like wearing an old pair of shoes— Caleb made her feel most uncomfortable, and in ways she tried not to think about! 'I think it would be best if the two of us just went back to a business footing, with you as a parent and me as one of the women who cares for your child.'

'Has no one ever pointed out to you that with relationships you can never go backwards?' he returned bluntly. 'As it was impossible for Alicia and I to go back to professional respect and friendship after our honeymoon, so it's impossible for the two of us to simply have a business arrangement between us!'

She felt a lurch in the pit of her stomach at the mention of his relationship with his wife. He was right, of course; after the intimacy the two of them had shared last week, she could never treat him as just another one of the children's fathers.

'I suggest we try,' she told him abruptly, turning away again, making good her escape this time, although she was sure Caleb still stood at the gate watching her.

She heaved a sigh of relief once she was inside the house, leaning weakly back against the door. Goodness, she hoped Caleb wasn't in the area much longer; *too* much longer and she wasn't sure she would be able to keep this up. Because seeing him again today had shown her one thing: she didn't trust herself to be alone with him! He did annoy her—no matter what he might choose to think to the contrary!—but he also aroused passions and desire within her that she had never known with any man before. He—

'Has Caleb gone?'

She turned at the sound of Kate's voice, forcing herself to smile as she looked down the hallway to where her friend stood. 'Finally,' she acknowledged drily, moving away from the support of the door, relieved to find her legs were no longer shaking.

Kate looked at Cat consideringly as she walked towards her. 'Kitty tells me she's invited him to dinner tomorrow evening.'

'So it would seem,' Cat confirmed noncommittally. 'And he took one look at her and realised exactly who she is!' she added.

'Oh.' Kate frowned worriedly.

'Mmm,' Cat sighed. 'Kitty is, as usual, completely unconcerned. And Caleb hasn't said anything about it yet, either.' She hadn't given him a chance to! 'But he will,' she said with certainty; she might not know Caleb that well, but she knew him well enough to realise that!

'Do you think—? What are we going to do about it?' Kate continued to show her concern as the two of them went through to the kitchen.

'What are *you* going to do about it?' Cat corrected her pointedly. 'I'm sorry, Kate, but there is no way I can spend the evening in Caleb's company! Please don't ask.' She held up a silencing hand as Kate would have spoken. 'Just trust me when I tell you my presence at dinner tomorrow evening would make it uncomfortable for everyone.' But especially for her! She had told Caleb she had other plans, and she was going to make sure that she did. She didn't like to think what conclusion he would draw if she should look as if she had changed those plans!

'You know Kitty,' Kate remonstrated softly. 'She's the one you'll have to convince!'

'That's why you're going to back me up when I tell her I had already made plans to go out. Oh, yes, you are, Kate,' she insisted firmly as her friend pulled a face. 'Anyway, Kitty should have made sure we were all at home tomorrow evening before issuing the invitation.'

'I can't argue with that logic,' Kate soothed. 'But I'm not the one you have to convince!'

No, Kitty was. And the main problem with that wasn't going to be Kitty's anger—because Kitty wouldn't be angry! Instead she would be hurt and disappointed. And neither she nor Kate liked to inflict those feelings on the woman they both loved so much...

But there was no way, absolutely no way Cat could do anything else where tomorrow evening was concerned. She would not spend that time in Caleb's company. She just wouldn't do it!

CHAPTER TEN

'HELLO, Cat.'

'Hello—' She had turned to greet the child who had just arrived for their morning session, only to have the words catch and hold in her throat as she saw *who* it was, who had said hello so shyly. Adam! And he had *spoken*. His voice had been husky, and slightly hesitant, but he had definitely spoken to her!

Cat looked sharply at the tall man who stood silently at his son's side. Why hadn't Caleb told her last night? Because they had been too busy arguing, on one subject or another, for him to have had the chance to discuss Adam! Or to tell her that Adam was talking again...

'Good morning, Adam.' She had turned quickly away from the searching expression on Caleb's face, going down on her haunches so that she was on the same level as the little boy. 'Did you have a nice weekend away?'

It was probably best, she decided, if she didn't mention the fact that he was speaking again. Whatever had happened this weekend—and Caleb must have talked with Adam—the important thing was that the little boy had obviously broken through whatever emotional barrier he had been hiding behind. To draw attention to it, to recognise the change in him, would only bring it all back to him.

'I bet you had a lovely time with your cousin, didn't you?' she said in a jolly voice, part of her longing to pick him up in her arms and give a shout of triumph, and maybe to have Adam join in that shout. She didn't doubt that within a few days he would be as noisy as the other children were! She also knew that she wouldn't pick him up or give that shout, again wanting to draw as little attention to him as possible.

He wrinkled his nose. 'She's a girl,' he scorned.

Cat laughed heartily at his disgusted tone. 'So was I, once.' She ruffled his hair affectionately as she straightened. 'But we all grow up.' She looked straight at Caleb as he gave a barely concealed snort at her statement.

'And then men's problems really begin,' he murmured throatily so that only Cat could hear him.

'Kitty's nice,' Adam said slowly after several thoughtful seconds. 'We're coming to see you tonight, Cat,' he added with satisfaction.

Cat had been incensed by Caleb's deliberate mockery, but she turned to look at him questioningly now after Adam's last claim.

'Subject to hiring the babysitter, remember?' he said drily. 'The babysitter had already made arrangements to go to the cinema this evening with her boyfriend! We called in to see Kitty just now so that we could explain the situation to her, and she suggested an early dinner, and that I bring Adam along with me.'

Cat's face fell. Not because Caleb was bringing Adam with him this evening, but because he had just called in to see Kitty; they had spent years safeguarding the older woman's privacy, but this man just strolled around to see her whenever he felt like it!

'You'll be coming too, won't you, Cat?' Adam clasped her hand in both of his as he looked up at her imploringly.

'Kitty mentioned that it might be a problem,' Caleb put in softly, challengingly, as Cat looked dismayed by the little boy's pleading tone.

Caleb knew it was a problem, damn him! She had told him herself last night that she wouldn't be there this evening.

She sensed, even if it were only tacit, a conspiracy!

Kitty had merely looked disappointed at breakfast when Cat had told her she had to go out to a meeting this evening and so wouldn't be in for dinner, but Caleb had left her in no doubt how he felt about her supposed plans for the evening...!

However, with Adam looking up at her so appealingly, those dark brown eyes—Alicia's eyes?—so widely innocent of guile, it was difficult to stick to her fictitious other plans. Perhaps with Adam's presence to alleviate any awkwardness—or any questions regarding Kitty's past!—tonight wouldn't be the strain she had imagined it would be...

'My plans have fallen through.' She met Caleb's mocking gaze unflinchingly. 'So yes, Adam—' she smiled down at the little boy '—I shall be at home tonight, after all.'

Adam beamed his pleasure, releasing her hand to look across to where the other children were playing.

'Go and join your friends, Adam,' his father suggested. 'I'll see you later.'

The two of them watched as Adam went shyly over to join the other children, none of them seeming in the least surprised when he spoke to them—just as they hadn't when he'd remained silent—simply including him in their game.

'Children seem to take most things in their stride,' Cat said wistfully as she turned back to Caleb.

'*You* didn't. When your cousin came to stay,' he reminded her as she looked puzzled.

This man remembered—and knew!—too much! 'That was sibling rivalry.' She grimaced. 'A totally different thing.'

'I suppose so,' Caleb accepted slowly. 'But I don't suppose your plans have fallen through for tomorrow evening too, have they?' He paused and took a deep breath. 'Because Jane doesn't have somewhere else to go tomorrow evening! And it would be nice if the two of us went out for a meal together.'

Did she want to go out with this man? The answer to that had to be a firm no! But she *did* want to hear about the transformation that had taken place in Adam…

Enough to spend an evening in Caleb's company…?

'We have several things we need to discuss,' Caleb added gently.

She could guess what one of those 'things' was! 'I—'

'I suggest we talk about this later, Cat,' Caleb told her smoothly as two mothers arrived to drop off their children for the day. 'But think about my suggestion, hmm?' he encouraged, turning away, giving the two women a charming smile before going out into the sunshine.

'It's a pity more of the fathers don't drop off their children,' one of the women said archly.

'Especially if they're as good-looking as that one!' The other woman giggled girlishly.

Cat, to her dismay, found she was deeply irritated by the exchange. How dared they talk about Caleb in that—familiar way?

Maybe they wouldn't have done if he hadn't smiled at them the way he had. He had—

She was jealous!

She shook her head in self-disgust. She was jealous of the fact that Caleb had smiled at two other women?

What was happening to her? Since Caleb had entered her life just over a week ago, she had been transformed herself, from a happy-go-lucky single woman—who was determined to remain so!—into a green-eyed monster who resented him even smiling at other women!

She had fallen in love with him…

'Are you okay, Cat?' A concerned Kate came over to look at her anxiously. 'You've gone very pale.'

She looked at Kate dazedly. Pale? She should have gone white!

Caleb Reynolds was not a man she should fall in love with. For one thing, he could be gone from the area in a matter of weeks. And where would that leave her? In exactly the same emotional turmoil she was in now—except Caleb wouldn't be around to see it.

Madness. Utter and complete—

'Cat?' Kate still looked at her worriedly.

She wasn't the only one, Cat realised; the two mothers were still waiting to leave their young children!

Caleb hadn't just thrown her emotions into turmoil, he was starting to affect her work—and that she wouldn't allow. 'Sorry, I was miles away,' she apologised.

'It happens to me all the time,' one of the other women sympathised. 'I was stopped for speeding the other day, and when the policeman asked me, in that patronising tone they adopt sometimes, what I had thought I was doing, I told him I was thinking about cooking a chicken for tea!' She raised her eyes heavenwards. 'But he meant, of course, what speed did I think I had been doing! Luckily for me, he saw the funny side of it!'

'And the speeding ticket?' Cat enquired, relieved to have the attention taken away from herself.

'He let me off with a warning.' The woman gave a gleeful smile. 'And hoped I enjoyed my dinner!'

It was such a ridiculous story that Cat knew it had to be a true one, and she joined in the general laughter, relieved on her part at having the attention diverted from her own lapse.

And it was a lapse she didn't allow to recur during the rest of the day, putting Caleb—and any feelings she might or might not have towards him—totally out of her mind. He was becoming a nuisance, if nothing else, and when she had the time she intended sitting back and putting all of this into perspective.

When she had the time. Which didn't look like being for a while yet. By the time the last child had been collected at the end of the day, and everything had been cleared away, it was time to go through and help Kitty with the preparations for dinner. A dinner now meant for five rather than just the four of them...

The menu had been decided on to fit in with their youngest guest—melon with strawberries to start, chicken for their main course, and chocolate meringue for dessert, with the standby of ice-cream for Adam, if he should happen not to like meringue.

Cat took on the task of scooping out the melon balls from inside the juicily ripe fruit, ready for putting them together with the strawberries.

'I'm so glad you changed your mind about joining us, after all,' Kitty told her warmly as she and Kate saw to the vegetables.

Cat gave her a resigned smile. 'A three-year-old charmer is hard to resist!'

Kitty laughed softly. 'But what about your meeting?'

Cat glanced across at Kate, and then back to Kitty, the same look of innocent query in both their faces. 'Next time I make up an excuse I'll make sure it's something vitally important—and just as urgent!' she told them wryly.

'I don't know what your problem is, Cat,' Kitty shrugged, returning to peeling the potatoes. 'Caleb is a very charming man, and far too polite, I'm sure, to refer to my past career unless one of us brings up the subject first.'

Which they wouldn't do!

'Besides,' Kitty went on teasingly, 'you had dinner on your own with him in his cottage last week!'

That was the major problem now for Cat when she thought about this evening. At least, it was the fact that she had been alone with him and had been kissed by him, had kissed him in return, that was the problem!

'It isn't as if he's still married or anything,' Kitty continued. 'It's all right, Cat,' she assured her as Cat frowned. 'I haven't broken any confidences; he told me himself this morning about his wife having died in the car accident.'

Making Cat wonder exactly how long those few minutes when Caleb and Adam had called in to see Kitty had actually lasted! Certainly long enough for Caleb's marital status to have come into the conversation!

'But you already knew about that, Kitty,' Cat reminded her softly.

'Well, of course I did,' she agreed. 'But, nevertheless, I thought it was—gentlemanly of him to reassure me. Very proper,' she concluded with satisfaction.

Cat did not associate the word 'gentlemanly' with Caleb, and as for the word 'proper'…!

And she certainly didn't like the idea of Caleb reassuring Kitty about anything; Kitty knew her well enough, trusted her enough, not to have had dinner with a married man!

But there was always the possibility that Caleb had done it for another reason, that he had wanted to know exactly how much she had told Kitty about him. That was much more likely than Kitty's version! Caleb was not a man who would relish having his personal life discussed, even less so where things he had obviously told Cat in confidence were concerned.

Well, he needn't worry on that score where she was involved. What he had told her last week about his marriage would go no further than herself; it was far too personal to talk about with any third party, even Kitty or Kate.

Cat gave a dismissive laugh now. 'I don't think you have Caleb Reynolds weighed up at all, Kitty.'

'I'm sure he has his faults. As we all do,' Kitty said steadily. 'But I still believe him to be an honest man.'

Too honest, on occasion, Cat readily agreed. But that was entering into subjects she would rather not discuss, deeming this an appropriate moment to absent herself from the kitchen on the pretext of changing for dinner.

The weather was still amazingly warm, but because Kitty insisted on formality when they had guests Cat chose to change into a sleeveless black fitted dress that reached just above her knee, her bare legs slender and tanned from the hours she had spent in the garden, the heels on her black shoes adding a little to her diminutive height. She brushed her curling red hair until it shone like burnished copper. Her reflection in the bedroom mirror showed her as slender and elegant, the dress giving her an air of sophistication that was usually absent. She only hoped she could maintain that air—she was going to need it!

Caleb and Adam were already in the sitting-room with Kitty when Cat arrived downstairs a few minutes later. As Cat had already known they were, having heard Caleb's car arrive outside a short time ago.

Caleb looked tall and handsome in a charcoal-grey suit, white shirt and discreetly patterned tie, Adam was a miniature of him, minus the formality of the jacket. Singly, the two Reynolds males were pretty potent stuff, but as a pair their appeal was quite lethal!

'Ah, Cat.' Kitty stood up, looking lovely in her fitted blue dress. 'I've already seen to Adam and Caleb's drinks, but please help yourself to a glass of wine.' She indicated the bottle of white wine she had opened for their guest; Adam had been supplied with a glass of orange juice. 'Kate is on the telephone, and I really must go and check on the chicken.' She made her apologies before leaving the room.

The silence, as the saying went, was deafening once Kitty had made her exit in a cloud of her favourite perfume. Cat frantically searched for something neutral to talk about, very aware of Caleb's brooding gaze as he stood across the sitting-room watching her. She couldn't think of a thing to say, her mind a complete blank!

'You look pretty.'

If the father had made that comment, Cat knew, no matter what her earlier resolve, that she would have become a trembling mass of feminine confusion. But it was Adam who had spoken so enthusiastically like a grown-up about her appearance.

She grinned across at him. 'So do you,' she told him happily.

'Hey, young man,' Caleb chided lightly as he crossed the room to Cat's side, 'find your own girl!' He draped an arm about her shoulders.

His words were so unexpected, let alone that possessive arm about her, that it took Cat several seconds to gather her scattered wits together. She was not Caleb's girl! And he certainly shouldn't say things like that in front of his young, impressionable son…!

She moved away from the curve of Caleb's arm, ostensibly so that she could talk to Adam, but mainly so that she could begin breathing again. This was only the beginning of the evening!

'Adam saw me first,' she said, giving the little boy a conspiratorial wink.

'I didn't really,' Adam accepted shyly. 'But you can't be Daddy's girl,' he added with certainty.

'I can't?' Cat prompted curiously.

'He's too old,' the little boy pronounced knowingly.

Cat tried to stop the bubble of laughter from escaping, but she made the mistake of glancing up at Caleb's darkly frowning expression, and the laughter just became too much for her.

Too old for her! There could only be thirteen or fourteen years' difference in their ages, and yet, to three-year-old Adam, his dad seemed ancient.

Caleb glared at his son, but it was obvious by the twitching of his lips, and the glittering humour in his eyes, that he was having trouble not laughing himself. 'Cat will be an old woman by the time you're old enough to marry her,' he teased Adam as he ruffled his hair affectionately.

'That's okay,' Adam insisted stubbornly. 'I—'

'Sorry about that.' Kate breezed into the room, smiling brightly. 'Do you all have a drink?' She moved to pour wine for herself and Cat when she realised they were the only two without a drink.

Cat was grateful for the interruption to a conversation that, although light-hearted on the surface, had an underlying seriousness the two adults had both been aware of. The subject had not been to Cat's liking at all!

She also, as the next few minutes were taken up with Kate chattering away inanely, found her friend's behaviour rather strange. She looked across at her searchingly. Kate's eyes were feverish, and there was a flush to her cheeks, and her brightness of mood definitely seemed forced.

Who had Kate been talking to on the telephone...?

Kate gave a barely perceptible shake of her head as she saw Cat looking at her, launching into a conversation about the exceptionally good weather they had been having.

Yes, Cat decided, there was definitely something wrong with Kate. Whoever she had been talking to on the telephone had upset her. No—not upset her exactly, Cat decided; disturbed would be a better description. Who on earth—?

'Dinner is served,' Kitty announced from the doorway, meaning the mystery of Kate's phone call, and the effect it had had on her, would have to wait until later.

They made an odd party for dinner, Cat decided as they walked through to the dining-room; three generations, almost like a family...

Cat shied away from such an idea. After the recent conversation with Caleb and Adam, it was more than a disturbing idea!

'We're a man short, of course,' Kitty observed as she organised the seating arrangements. 'Ordinarily I would have put you, Caleb, as the senior male present— Did I say something funny?' She looked up with mild query as Caleb chuckled and Cat smiled.

'Nothing of importance,' Caleb easily replied as he and Cat sobered.

Cat deliberately didn't meet the look he wanted to share across the table with her. She didn't want any shared jokes with him; it only added to the intimacy between them, and it was that she was trying to dispel!

'In the circumstances, I thought it best,' Kitty continued as if the incident had never happened, 'that I sit at the head of the table, with Cat and Adam on one side, and Kate and Caleb on the other. If that suits everyone?'

It was preferable, Cat decided, to having Caleb seated next to her. At least, she thought it was, until she found herself facing him across the width of the table. Wonderful! It was guaranteed to make her lose her appetite.

Or, it would have done, if the doorbell hadn't rung at that moment…!

'How inconvenient.' Kitty frowned her irritation with the interruption.

Kate sat forward. 'I'll go—'

'No, I will.' Cat stilled her friend as she would have got up.

Kate protested, 'But—'

'I promise I'll be back before the food gets cold,' Cat told Kitty laughingly, deliberately not looking at Caleb as she left the room, although she was aware he was watching her.

Kitty might find this interruption irksome, but Cat didn't mind at all. It was going to be a long enough evening any-

way, with Caleb sitting across the table from her looking
so handsome, his gaze compelling—no matter how she
might try to avoid it! Yes, it was going to be a very long
evening; a few minutes' respite wouldn't do Cat any harm
whatsoever! In fact—

'Toby!' she greeted in some surprise as she opened the
door to find him standing there.

He had been gone almost a week now, and she had been
starting to wonder if he could possibly have gone for good.
It wouldn't have been very polite of him to do so without
saying goodbye to them all, not after all the meals they had
shared together, but she knew he could be temperamental,
so that was no guarantee that he hadn't left.

'Don't look so surprised to see me, Cat,' Toby said at
her stunned expression. 'I telephoned earlier and spoke to
Kate,' he added huskily.

Toby was the person who had been talking to Kate on
the telephone earlier...? The person who had disturbed her
friend? But what on earth could Toby have said to Kate to
have caused that reaction?

'Well?' Toby looked down at her with raised brows.
'You don't usually keep me standing on the doorstep, Cat.'

And he didn't usually upset Kate. In fact, she could never
remember anyone having done that in quite this way before...

Could she invite him in when they were about to sit
down to dinner? Even if one of their guests was the most
annoying man she had ever met? Although she had a feeling Kate could have already told Toby that earlier on the
telephone...

As she looked up at the determination in Toby's expression, Cat had a feeling she didn't really have a choice concerning inviting him in...

CHAPTER ELEVEN

'LOOK who's arrived!' Cat announced brightly as she re-entered the dining-room with Toby immediately behind her. 'It looks as if we aren't a man short, after all, Kitty,' she told her happily as the four people seated at the table just stared up at the two of them.

Kate, Cat could see, was perturbed by Toby's arrival, Kitty was over her surprise and now smiled up at Toby like the gracious hostess that she was, Adam looked mildly curious about this newcomer, and Caleb—Caleb didn't look in the least pleased by the other man's arrival, his gaze flinty, his expression darkly scowling.

Toby's jaw set, meeting the challenge in the other man's demeanour with amusement.

Great! It looked as if they were all in for an eventful meal, if nothing else!

Although Toby's unexpected entrance had definitely taken the strain off Cat; she had no doubt that these two men were more than capable of taking care of themselves if any verbal exchange did occur—and she had a feeling there could be several!

'Do sit down, Toby,' Kitty invited warmly, the charming Toby a favourite with her. 'Cat, could you lay another place opposite me—?'

'I'll do it,' Kate instantly offered, standing up very quickly to go out to the kitchen to get the necessary cutlery and glasses.

'I'll help her.' Cat followed her friend, knowing Kate couldn't manage to carry everything on her own. Besides, it was the perfect opportunity to talk to Kate...

137

'Why is he doing this?' Kate groaned as she stood in the middle of the kitchen, shaking her head. 'I told him earlier that we had guests for dinner. I don't understand him at all.'

'Does it matter?' Cat took the remaining half of melon out of the fridge, scooping out some melon balls and then preparing more strawberries.

Kate swallowed hard. 'I don't know. I—Toby has been acting strangely lately.'

Having prepared the melon and strawberries, Cat now took out the accompanying cutlery, Kate seeming too agitated to do any of it. 'He hasn't been here lately,' Cat said.

'I meant before that,' Kate replied. 'When he was here last. The night you went to talk to Caleb about Adam.'

Kate, usually calm, controlled Kate, was definitely in a state about something...

'In what way did he act strangely?' Cat asked slowly.

'He— Well, he—' Kate sighed impatiently. 'He kissed me!' she announced incredulously, as if she still couldn't quite believe it had happened.

'Toby—kissed—you...?' Cat wasn't just incredulous, she was stunned.

Toby always seemed rather in awe of Kate, her natural coolness of nature deterring him from behaving too outrageously or familiarly with her. But kissing her was certainly familiar! Kate was right, Toby was behaving strangely. But then, so was Kate—because until this moment she hadn't mentioned that kiss...

'It's all right, Cat, I'm sure it meant nothing,' Kate hastened to reassure her. 'He seemed angry that night when he arrived, and after a few minutes' conversation I gathered it was because he had met you earlier on your way to visit Caleb.' She swallowed hard once more. 'Anyway, after Kitty had gone to bed, he seemed reluctant to leave. I thought it was because he was waiting for you to come home. But then he—' She broke off uncomfortably.

'Kissed you,' Cat completed, looking searchingly at her friend. 'And how did you feel about that?' she prompted gently, Kate looking very agitated indeed now.

'I was naturally surprised. I— He had never given any indication—any impression— Of course, I knew he had done it because he was angry at you for being with Caleb, but—'

'Forget about that for the moment, Kate,' Cat advised. 'I asked how *you* felt about it,' she reminded her, the cutlery and glasses momentarily forgotten in the intensity of their conversation.

Uncertainty flickered across Kate's beautiful face. 'I— he—I—' She sat down abruptly at the kitchen table. 'I liked it, Cat!' she wailed, her face contorted into despair. 'In fact, I more than liked it! I've tried to put it out of my mind the last few days, to pretend it never happened, but when he telephoned earlier—! Just the sound of his voice—!' She let out a shaky breath.

'You're in love with him,' Cat realised dazedly. Kate and Toby…? She had never even imagined such a match!

'What am I going to do?' Kate cried, her calm defences completely shattered.

Cat sat down too, reaching out to take Kate's hands into her own. 'What do you want to do?' she enquired.

Kate and Toby… She would never have thought— They were so different! Toby was boyish and volatile, Kate so mature and composed. The attraction of opposites…? Why not; she and Caleb were completely different too, and yet there was definitely an attraction between the two of them!

'Carry on pretending it never happened,' Kate answered flatly. 'For all of us to be friends, as we were before.'

Cat shook her head regretfully. 'Someone told me yesterday that it's impossible to go backwards in a relation-ship,' she recalled.

'Caleb?'

'Caleb,' she confirmed ruefully. 'Do you really think you could just go back to being friends with Toby?' She looked searchingly at Kate, seeing the answer in her friend's mis-ery. 'What did he say to you on the telephone earlier, Kate?' she persisted. 'Does he want the two of you to go back to being friends?' Somehow she didn't think so. It was obvious now why Toby had disappeared so abruptly after that night. But the first person he had wanted to talk to when he came back was Kate...

'I don't know what he wants,' Kate confessed. 'I always thought it was you he—well, that he—'

Cat's dismissive laugh cut in on what she was trying to say. 'Toby and I don't mean anything to each other in that way,' she easily replied, having picked up on this miscon-ception of Kate's earlier in this conversation. She wanted Kate to know there never had been, and never would be, anything between herself and Toby; Kate had enough prob-lems dealing with how she felt, without mistakenly thinking that! 'Toby has always seemed like a mischievous brother to me!'

Kate frowned. 'But you and he have always got on so well together—'

'Too well,' she smiled. 'There's absolutely no spark be-tween us, no male/female thing at all.' Although she was still finding it difficult to accept that it existed between Kate and Toby... But she would definitely get used to the idea. 'I think—'

'Is everything okay out here, ladies?' Caleb appeared in the kitchen doorway, his narrowed gaze quickly taking in the fact that they were both sitting at the kitchen table rather than getting on with the job they had come out here to do. 'Kitty was concerned.' He explained his own presence.

Cat gave Kate's hand a last reassuring squeeze as she stood up. 'We're coming now,' she answered Caleb breezily.

As she might have guessed, he took absolutely no notice of her, continuing to stand in the doorway.

'Make yourself useful,' Cat instructed, thrusting the two wine-glasses into his hands, then picking up the bowl containing the melon and strawberries before turning to look at Kate. 'Ready?' she queried encouragingly.

Kate drew in a deep breath before standing up determinedly. 'Ready,' she agreed, gathering up the silver cutlery.

Cat couldn't help her look of curiosity in Toby's direction as they went back into the dining-room; his guarded gaze was resting on Kate as she arranged the cutlery in front of him. She was right; Kate and Toby could never return to just friendship; they were circling around each other at the moment, not exactly adversaries, but certainly not comfortable in each other's company.

Exactly like Caleb and herself...

Cat glanced across the table at him as she sat down, not in the least surprised to find him looking straight back at her, one eyebrow raised questioningly. Well, it was a question she didn't have the answer to. And she very much doubted Kate was about to enlighten him either!

'This is so much better,' Kitty announced happily, seemingly unaware of any tension in the room.

She and Adam had to be the only ones that were! Kate was seated to Toby's right, her face stiffly averted as she ate her fruit, seeming not even to taste it. In fact, Cat doubted her friend even knew what she was eating.

As for Toby, he merely picked at the food, the laughing self-confidence he had displayed when he'd first arrived no longer in evidence as he shot Kate surreptitious glances from beneath dark lashes.

Cat herself was doing a good job of avoiding the steady eyes levelled across at her as she ate her own fruit, Caleb obviously feeling none of Toby's uncertainty as he openly watched her every move.

Kitty continued to smile happily. 'This is the first dinner party we've had in this house for—'

Cat's breath caught in her throat as Kitty paused, and she could see Kate turn sharply to look at her grandmother too, as they both waited for Kitty to complete the statement.

'More years than I care to think about,' Kitty finished lightly.

Kate's attention returned thankfully to her food, but Cat still held her breath, aware of the expectant silence that still surrounded them all.

'But I thought the three of you had only lived here three or four years?' Caleb put in mildly.

The silence had been filled. By Caleb. As Cat had known it would be. And exactly as she had guessed it would be; she had no doubt that he remembered exactly how long they had lived in this house!

But he knew who Kitty was; she had seen that knowledge in his face last night when he'd stood talking to her outside. As he had known then that Cat had realised he knew. Was he just playing games with them now? The mere idea of that made her angry.

'Three or four years *is* a long time,' she told him determinedly. 'In some cases—' she looked pointedly at Adam '—it's a lifetime!'

Caleb's mouth twisted derisively at the way she had turned the conversation back on him. 'So it is,' he accepted. 'I stand corrected.' He gave an apologetic inclination of his head in Kitty's direction.

She laughed. 'At my age, Caleb, three or four years can seem like for ever!' She shook her head. 'Everyone says that the time passes more swiftly the older you get, but I can assure you that isn't the case with me.' A slight frown marred her creamy brow.

Cat looked at her searchingly. She had never heard Kitty talk like this before, almost wistfully, as if there was so much she regretted...

And there was Kate, in turmoil because of her recently realised feelings for Toby...

Her own emotions weren't much better where Caleb was concerned!

The three of them had lived here quite happily for the past few years—or so she believed—but in the nine days since Caleb had arrived in the village that seemed to have changed, none of them quite happy with their lot in life any more. Where was it all going to end? That was what really bothered Cat...!

'So what are you doing in the area, Mr Reynolds?' Toby enquired in a brittle voice, the introductions obviously having been made by Kitty while Kate and Cat were out of the room.

Caleb paused in his eating, looking across at the other man with cool grey eyes. 'Very little—Mr Westward,' he drawled pointedly. 'You?'

'The same,' Toby returned guardedly. 'And I'm sure Kate and Cat—' he turned to include both of them in his smile '—can vouch for the fact I'm very good at it!'

'Very,' Cat was the one to answer drily, giving Kate the time she needed to be able to join in this conversation. 'And surely we can disperse with the formality of Mr? We're all friends here,' she added slightly untruthfully. Wary acquaintances would have been a far better description. Even Toby, whom she had thought she knew quite well as a friend, wasn't quite what she had thought him to be...

'But there must be some reason, Toby,' Caleb continued mildly, 'why you chose this area to come to and paint?'

Toby gave the other man a narrow-eyed look. 'It's a beautiful area,' he muttered.

Caleb gave an inclination of his head. 'I agree with you. But as I understand it you don't do landscapes?'

Now it was Cat's turn to look at Caleb sharply. Until a few days ago, when he had given her the impression he had never even heard of Toby, he had certainly known nothing about the other man's work, either. Obviously he had checked up on Toby since then...

Caleb met her accusing gaze with calm deliberation. So I checked him out, those mocking eyes seemed to say; it's a free world, isn't it?

'You're right, I don't,' Toby bit out tersely. 'When I said it was a beautiful area, I was, of course, referring to the peace and quiet to be found here. I've also appreciated how the village people respect one's privacy,' he added hardly, blue eyes fixed on the other man.

Ouch. Cat grimaced inwardly. If Caleb didn't particularly like Toby, then the feeling was surely reciprocated! Even Kitty, who liked calmness around her, couldn't help but pick up on the tension between the two men.

'Except for Lilley at the post office, of course,' Cat put in humorously before turning to Adam. 'How are you liking your melon and strawberries, Adam?' Of the six of them, the little boy was the only one who hadn't picked up on the tension—coming from several different areas! He was contentedly eating the fruit in his bowl, the port wine having been omitted from his portion.

'It's very nice, thank you,' he said in his best polite voice, suddenly shy at being singled out for attention in this way.

But it was the break in the conversation needed to dispel some of the tension, Kitty stepping in to talk of subjects that were less controversial. Although, considering how sensitive the majority of people at the table appeared to be, that wasn't quite as easy as it should have been, either!

But they managed to limp through the first course of the meal, Cat and Kate offering to clear the bowls away and serve the main course.

'This is just awful!' Kate groaned her relief at being in the relative peace of the kitchen.

'I'm treating it like a trip to the dentist,' Cat grinned as she stacked the dishwasher. 'Something to be got through!'

'And am I an extraction, or just a filling?' Caleb joined in as he entered the kitchen with a dish they had missed earlier in their haste to escape.

He was actually turning out to be neither of those things; it was the morose silence Toby seemed to have fallen into that was creating most of the problem. He was usually a tease, joking and laughing with all of them, so his silence now was noticeable; even Kitty had shot him one or two concerned glances in the last ten minutes.

'Actually——' Cat straightened '——it's the needle in the gum in both those cases that I'm particularly averse to!' She looked at him challengingly, green eyes dancing with humour.

'In that case——' Caleb leant casually back against one of the kitchen units '——I'll opt to be a filling——at least you get to keep the tooth!'

She wasn't particularly certain she liked the implication behind that comment, but this wasn't the time to argue the point. 'At this rate,' she muttered as she served the chicken onto the plates, 'there will be more of us in the kitchen than there are in the dining-room!'

'It's cosier in here, anyway.' Caleb picked up one of the slivers of carrot Kate was tipping into a serving dish.

Cat looked across at him. 'Should you have left Adam?' She frowned her concern; after all, it could only be days since the little boy had begun to talk again!

'Kitty was encouraging him to talk about his weekend away when I came out.' Caleb smiled. 'Westward's eyes had glazed over,' he added with satisfaction, giving Kate a searching look as, her hands shaking slightly, she tipped some of the carrots onto the work-top instead of into the serving dish. 'Or else he just has something else—or someone—on his mind...?' He raised questioning brows at Cat as Kate turned hurriedly away to deal with the potatoes. Too hurriedly, Caleb's expression told Cat.

She shook her head at him before placing the dish of carrots in his hands. 'Make yourself useful and take that through, would you?' she ordered. Help me, her eyes pleaded with him; help Kate!

'Certainly,' he accepted easily, that agreement meaning so much more than the taking in of the vegetables. It was there in his eyes, a sudden understanding.

How had Caleb realised so quickly what was going on, whereas she had actually needed Kate to tell her of her dilemma before she understood? Cat wondered as they completed putting the food in the serving dishes before taking it into the dining-room. Then she berated herself; would she allow the man to do anything right? She knew the answer to that all too well; her emotions, the way she felt about him, wouldn't let her!

But she couldn't fault Caleb's behaviour during the rest of the meal; he flattered Kitty shamelessly, teased Adam, talked conversationally with Toby about London, spoke gently to Kate about the kittens and how they were doing. If Cat had any fault to find it was that he didn't so much as glance her way during that whole time, let alone flatter, tease or talk to her!

She wanted it all ways, she scolded herself as they ate the delicious chocolate meringue Kitty had made earlier in the day, looking across the table at Caleb from beneath lowered lashes. Damn the man. Damn him to—— He was laughing at her! she realised. Not openly, not with his mouth, but those grey eyes as they looked into hers were full of it.

'Coffee.' She stood up abruptly, again needing to escape for a few minutes.

Kitty looked up at her, mildly surprised. 'We haven't finished dessert yet—'

'I'll just put it on to percolate,' she insisted desperately. 'That way it will be ready when we've finished eating.' She hurried from the room before any more objections could be raised.

She stumbled into the kitchen. She felt like crying. Ridiculous. How utterly ridiculous. What was wrong with her?

What was she going to do about loving Caleb?

'Cat...?'

She turned sharply at the sound of Toby's voice, her eyes swimming with the tears she refused to let fall. 'It's all your fault,' she lashed out at him irrationally, her anger really directed at Caleb, but as he wasn't here...! 'What on earth have you done to Kate?'

A shutter instantly came down over Toby's boyishly handsome features. 'I think that's between Kate and me, don't you?' he returned stiffly.

'As it happens, no, I don't!' Cat snapped accusingly. 'You have no right to play with her emotions!'

'And what makes you think I'm playing?' he demanded with quiet intensity.

'Because I'm not sure you're capable of being serious,' she told him scathingly. 'You were acting like a jealous protector towards me only last week—'

'And I still don't trust Reynolds,' he growled.

'You don't even know him—'

'And neither do you!' Toby insisted as he moved further into the kitchen. 'Oh, I'll admit that he can be charming, likeable even, but at the same time he gives little of his real self away—'

'So, apparently, do you!' she returned heatedly.

Toby grew suddenly still, looking at her with puzzled blue eyes. 'What do you mean by that?'

What did she mean? Not, she decided slowly, what Toby thought she meant... What did he think she meant? Oh, why, she cried inwardly again, had everything become so complicated? They had all been fine, bumbling along in their own little way, the house in order, the playschool a success, and suddenly it was all such a muddle; Kate was in love with this complex man standing across the room, and she—

'Am I interrupting something?' Caleb questioned harshly from the open doorway.

And she was in love with Caleb, a man who, as Toby had just said, gave little of his real self away!

CHAPTER TWELVE

'NOT in the least,' Toby answered the other man casually, giving Cat one last searching look before turning away. 'It seems there's no coffee made yet for me to help with.' He indicated the percolating coffee, obviously his excuse for being here at all.

Caleb's eyes remained suspicious as he picked up on the atmosphere between Cat and Toby—and obviously wondered at the reason for it. 'I've decided not to stay for coffee,' he told Cat hardly. 'Adam is almost falling asleep in his chair and I need to get him home to bed. So it will be coffee for only four, I'm afraid.'

'Better make that three,' Toby put in tautly. 'I have to be going too,' he explained at Cat's accusing look in his direction.

He wasn't going anywhere until he had explained himself! He had forced his presence on them this evening. For his own reasons! And now he was leaving again without any word of explanation. Again, Cat felt, for his own reasons! It just wasn't good enough. Poor Kate had been a nervous wreck ever since Toby's telephone call earlier, and it had been his choice to barge in on their dinner party. He owed Kate, at least, some sort of explanation for his behaviour, if nothing else.

'Stay a while longer, Toby.' Cat moved to put her hand on his arm. 'It isn't as if you have to hurry home to feed the dog or anything.'

'Or put the baby to bed!' Caleb added harshly, grey gaze flinty as it swept over Cat and Toby as they now stood so close together, scowling as he turned abruptly away to walk back down the hallway to the dining-room.

'Caleb—'

'Leave him, Cat,' Toby cut in harshly. 'He's had enough for one evening, too!'

She blinked up at him, the hand she had reached out towards Caleb falling limply back to her side. 'Enough of what?' she said dazedly, shaking her head, red curls bouncing. 'You know, Toby, I haven't just lost the plot—I don't think I ever had it!'

'Oh, I had it,' he returned, 'but I've certainly lost it!' He turned away. 'Your guests appear to be leaving,' he turned back to tell her drily as Caleb appeared in the hallway carrying a sleepy Adam in his arms.

Caleb wasn't her guest, he was Kitty's, but nevertheless she knew what Toby meant, and the next five minutes or so were taken up with saying goodnight to Caleb and a very tired Adam.

It wasn't until after they had left that Cat realised Caleb had made no further mention of taking her out to dinner the following evening...

She had been going to accept too!

Cool didn't even begin to describe Caleb's attitude when he dropped Adam off at playschool the following morning; icy summed it up so much better!

There was none of the warmth and teasing of yesterday morning, and no mention of their dinner together this evening, despite the fact that yesterday he had said they would discuss it again later. Instead Caleb was cold and withdrawn, spoke briefly to Adam before nodding abruptly to Cat and turning to leave.

But Cat wanted to talk to him about Adam, needed to know— Well, she needed to know several things...!

And so she did something she had thought she would never do. 'Caleb!' she called after him softly as she followed him out into the hallway, her mouth going suddenly dry as he turned back to her enquiringly, one dark brow raised over those cold grey eyes. 'I believe...' she paused to moisten lips that had suddenly become dry too '...that we have a dinner engagement this evening?'

Her chin went up challengingly as she met his gaze. Although inwardly she was quaking. If he should say no—! Now she had some idea of how a man must feel when he asked a woman for a date—and it wasn't much fun!

His mouth thinned. 'I was wrong,' he said slowly.

She felt the blood drain from her flushed cheeks, her eyes huge in the sudden paleness of her face. He couldn't— He wouldn't—

'I don't dislike having a woman asking me for a date after all.' He grinned good-humouredly. 'I thought I would,' he ruminated, 'but, actually, it makes a pleasant change!'

She wasn't asking him for a date, damn him, she was reminding him he had asked her for one! 'You—'

'Especially if *you're* the woman doing the asking,' he ended huskily—completely robbing Cat of speech!

He had seemed so angry when he left last night, but then none of them—Adam excluded—had been relaxed. In fact, it had been a strained evening all round, Toby taking his leave minutes after Caleb and Adam, the three women left to drink the coffee. Only Kitty had seemed to feel like talking then, Kate presumably lost in thoughts of Toby, Cat immersed in her own particular misery.

Not that she felt too much happier at this moment, no longer sure who had done the asking about dinner this evening!

Caleb reached out a hand and lightly touched her cheek.

'I'll call for you around seven-thirty. We can decide then where we would like to eat.'

Cat had flinched slightly as he'd touched her, moving completely away from him as several parents entered with their children. 'That will be fine, Mr Reynolds,' she assured him briskly.

'See you later—Cat,' he returned, grey eyes openly mocking her suddenly businesslike manner.

Cat had to force herself to concentrate on her work for the rest of the day, her attention constantly wandering to Caleb and the evening they were to spend together. It was something that had never happened to her before, and by the end of what had seemed a very long day she felt more than a little irritated with Caleb for being the cause of her inattentiveness.

Which didn't bode well for their evening together!

'Well, this makes a pleasant change.' Kitty beamed at her when told that Cat wouldn't be in for dinner tonight because she was meeting Caleb. 'Both my girls—' she put an arm about both Cat and Kate's shoulders '—going off for the evening with a man. I was beginning to despair of the two of you!' she admitted ruefully.

'Toby just telephoned,' Kate explained as Cat looked at her questioningly. 'I— He asked me to join him at his cottage for dinner,' she confessed awkwardly, a bright flush to her cheeks.

This was a Kate that Cat had never seen before, slightly apprehensive, but at the same time inwardly excited. Though it was far from the first time Kate had been involved with a man; she'd been very popular when they were at university, but she had never been in this emotional state about any of them. Cat only hoped Toby proved to be worth it. If he hurt Kate…!

'That will be nice,' she encouraged. 'So you're going to be on your own this evening, Kitty?'

'Who knows?' the older woman returned with a sparkle in her blue eyes. 'Maybe I'll find a man of my own to spend the evening with!'

They all laughed at the idea of that. Kitty had been happily married for twenty years before the early death of her husband, and there had been no other men in her life since. What she had had with her Dan, she claimed, could never be equalled...

'I feel more than a little silly.' Kate grimaced at Cat an hour later when she came downstairs ready for her dinner date with Toby, her dress the same deep blue as her eyes, revealing long tanned legs, her only make-up a peach lip-gloss, her hair loose and silkily blonde about her shoulders.

'You look lovely,' Cat told her warmly.

'But it's only Toby,' Kate replied, a flush still in her cheeks, saying it wasn't 'only' at all!

Once again Cat telepathically pleaded with Toby not to hurt Kate. Because it was obvious to Cat now that Kate— even to her own surprise!—was in love with him. But with Toby it was impossible to tell how he felt, let alone if he was being serious.

He had better be serious, Cat decided fiercely. Although there was that mysterious blonde he had been seen with a few weeks ago... No, Cat refused to accept that he might just be playing with Kate. If it turned out that he was, he would have Cat to answer to!

In the meantime, she had her own date to think about. Just thinking of spending an evening out with Caleb filled her with nervous tension. One minute he was warm and friendly—in fact, more than warm, and definitely more than friendly!—and the next he was cold and distant. In truth, neither state filled her with a sense of well-being. But she had been the one to instigate spending this evening with him, and so she would just have to get through it as best she could.

Kate had already left, and Kitty had disappeared somewhere too, when the doorbell rang at exactly seven-thirty, leaving Cat to open the door to Caleb herself. She checked her appearance one last time in the hall mirror before going to the door; she was wearing a short emerald-green fitted dress, her hair deeply red against its colour, her overall appearance tanned and healthy.

Her breath caught in her throat as she looked at Caleb in pale grey shirt and black trousers, the darkness of his hair still damp from the shower he must have taken before coming out.

'Are you going to invite me in?' he drawled as she stood and stared at him. 'Or do you keep all your dates standing on the doorstep?'

She didn't usually have dates so she couldn't really answer that question!

But she did open the door wider for him to come inside, leading the way to the sitting-room, able to feel his gaze on her as she walked down the hallway, making her very aware of the sway of her hips and the length of her bare, tanned legs.

'Would you like a drink?' Cat offered once they reached the sitting-room.

'Better not,' Caleb said. 'I'm driving, and I would like a glass of wine with our meal.'

Then why come in at all? Cat wanted to say. But didn't… Afraid of what his answer might be?

'Kate has gone out,' she excused. 'And Kitty seems to have disappeared too.'

'To Rose Cottage,' Caleb nodded. 'Didn't she tell you she was babysitting Adam this evening?' he mused as Cat frowned her surprise. 'Jane had something else planned this evening after all, and the only other person I could think of leaving Adam with was Kitty. Luckily she was pleased to do it.'

Which explained Kitty's earlier remark about finding a man of her own to spend the evening with!

But it also meant that Kitty had known even before Cat had mentioned it to her that she was going out with Caleb this evening! 'No doubt she'll enjoy herself,' Cat said with certainty. 'In fact, they probably both will.'

Caleb agreed. 'They were playing animal snap when I left.'

'She used to play—' Cat broke off as she realised exactly what she had been about to say.

'Yes?' Caleb persisted softly, brows raised questioningly.

She had been about to speak completely out of turn! Such was the effect Caleb had on her. They had spent years protecting Kitty, and she had almost—

'Kitty used to play cards years ago,' she dismissed quickly. 'Although I don't think it was snap!' she added affectionately.

Caleb relaxed, holding up her black jacket for her to put on as she picked up her handbag in preparation for leaving. 'Adam has the memory of an elephant. He never forgets,' he explained drily. 'I used to think I would give him a fighting chance—but he wiped the floor with me half a dozen times before I realised he didn't need any help!'

'I shouldn't worry; Kitty will only make that mistake once,' Cat assured him as they went outside to his car.

Adam was definitely a safe subject for them to discuss, both of them visibly relaxing. Although, as Cat noted the now smiling Caleb, it was the first time she had realised he had been tense when he'd arrived...! The trouble with

Caleb was that he always gave the impression of being totally in control, of himself and any situation he found himself in, so it was difficult to imagine him ever being less than sure about anything. But he had been unsure about the initial meeting with her this evening...

He shrugged now. 'I try to only make a mistake once,' he told her harshly.

Like marriage, Cat realised.

As she was supposed to realise?

Was Caleb trying to warn her off having any thoughts of a serious relationship where he was concerned?

Well, he needn't have any such worries about her; she might have made the mistake of falling in love with him, but she certainly had no thoughts of marrying him! Graham's complete betrayal of her five years ago had ensured she would only make that mistake once!

'I think it best, if possible, not to make the mistake in the first place,' she returned frostily. 'Where were you thinking of going this evening?' She changed the subject as he turned the ignition on the car and drove away from the pavement.

'Unless you have other preferences, I was told that the pub about two miles down this road is rather good, and that we don't have to book,' he said, the latter obviously the key factor here.

Although Cat didn't think too many restaurants would be fully booked on a Tuesday evening! But the pub suited her just fine.

'The Swan,' she returned. 'It's very good.' Although she couldn't help wondering who he had got his advice from. If it had been Kitty, then it wasn't a problem, but if he should have asked someone like Lilley—!

'Jane, actually,' he offered with a smile, seeming to read

her thoughts, grey eyes filled with laughter as he gave her a brief glance.

'Fine.' Cat sank back in her seat.

'You surprised me this morning, you know,' Caleb told her a few minutes later when they entered the pub lounge, quite a few of the tables already busy, although they still managed to find one that looked out over the garden at the back.

She didn't need two guesses to know in what way she had surprised him! Well, he needn't worry; he wasn't the only one that was surprised at her forwardness in reminding him of their date!

'You didn't seem surprised,' she muttered as she glanced at the menu. Deliberately so. Now that they were seated, the other diners all strangers to her, she was having trouble looking at Caleb at all!

He definitely stood out in a crowd. Any crowd! He was so tall and dark, his handsomeness having drawn several female heads in their direction when they'd walked in. But Cat didn't need any reminding of how attractive he was, was too aware of it already!

'Pleasantly surprised,' he rejoined, smiling broadly across at her now, seeming completely unaware of the female interest he was still attracting. 'I thought you were never going to ask,' he added teasingly.

Her eyes flashed deeply green. 'Don't hold your breath; it will never happen again!' she clipped, determined to try to rebuild some of the barrier she tried to keep between herself and this man. Fragile as it might be! 'You said you would tell me what happened with Adam,' she reminded him; she didn't want Caleb to think she actually wanted to spend time in his company. That would never do!

'I'll go and order our food first,' he said. 'We may as well eat while we talk.' He stood up to go to the bar.

'It should be my treat, really.' Cat looked up at him with a pensive smile.

Caleb didn't return her smile. 'When I can't afford to pay will be the time you can!' he rasped harshly.

She couldn't see that being anywhere in the near future; Caleb gave every indication of being quite a wealthy man!

'Prawn salad,' she requested.

'Drink?' he asked stiffly.

She really did seem to have struck a raw nerve. That was the problem with people who had been married or in a serious relationship before—you never knew when you were going to step into a minefield. Although, she admitted, she wasn't without prickles herself.

'A glass of white wine would be nice. Unless you would like me to drive back?'

'Have you ever driven an automatic before?'

Prickles were one thing, condescension was something else! 'As it happens, yes,' she bit out; her father had an automatic four-wheel drive that he drove around the farm, and Cat had driven it dozens of times.

Caleb gave a mocking inclination of his head. 'In that case, I'll bear your offer in mind.' He walked over to the bar to place their order, his opening comment—whatever it was—earning him an appreciative laugh from the barmaid.

Arrogant. Condescending—! If he thought his flirtatious behaviour with Hayley was going to have any effect on her, he was wrong; she had known Hayley for a couple of years now, knew that her husband, a builder, had been known to go in with his fists flying if he thought one of the customers was being too friendly with his wife. And the way Cat felt about him right now it wouldn't do Caleb any harm whatsoever to receive a punch on the nose!

Caleb returned a couple of minutes later carrying a tray

containing two glasses of white wine, and a bowl of marie rose sauce. 'Apparently you like to put your own sauce on the prawns,' he said drily.

'Thank you.' Cat accepted the glass of wine and bowl of sauce he placed in front of her, barely able to conceal her smile of satisfaction.

Caleb relaxed back in his seat, but not opposite her this time, preferring to sit at Cat's side on the upholstered bench-seat. 'You've been here lots of times before,' he said conversationally.

She sipped her wine. 'Sometimes, at the end of a long week, when none of us can be bothered to cook, we come down here for a treat,' she replied.

'Just the three of you?'

She met his narrowed gaze unblinkingly. 'Without exception.'

'"All for one, and one for all",' he quoted.

She raised one auburn brow. 'Is there something wrong with that?'

He shrugged. 'It's just unusual, that's all. Two young women living with the grandmother of one of them,' he explained as Cat continued to look at him.

'It's a large house,' she dismissed easily, once again forcing herself to relax. 'I thought we were going to talk about Adam?' She certainly had no intention of discussing further what he considered their unusual living arrangements! Besides, she had never thought of them as such...

Caleb looked preoccupied. 'Before we get on to the subject of Adam, I think I owe you an apology from a few minutes ago.' He sighed. 'Alicia came from a wealthy family,' he explained suddenly. 'I was more than capable of financially taking care of my wife and child, but she never let me forget the fact that she was quite capable of taking care of herself and Adam without any help from me!'

For a man as proud as Caleb, that couldn't have been an easy situation either. Well, the truth was, Cat came from a wealthy family too, and she didn't need any financial support from anyone either, but her mother had taught her long ago that there was such a thing as male pride, and, once damaged, it was virtually irreparable.

She grinned up at Caleb. 'I'm more than happy to let you buy me a meal,' she assured him playfully.

'But nothing else,' he realised ruefully, leaning back on the bench-seat. 'I hope you aren't the sort of woman that gloats, Cat...?' He smiled.

She showed her puzzlement. 'Not that I'm aware of—'

'I was only joking,' he assured her laughingly, reaching out to lightly squeeze her hand. And then forgot to let it go again... 'You were one hundred per cent right about Adam,' he said, sobering. 'He did overhear the argument between his mother and me. And after his mother had driven away with him in the back of the car he cried for me. He wanted his daddy,' Caleb said grimly. 'Alicia became angry—upset, Adam told me. She wanted him to stop saying it. But Adam didn't stop, and the angrier she became, the more he kept asking for me. And then Alicia crashed the car...' He shuddered as he relived Adam's tortured, guilt-ridden silence of the last six months.

Because Adam had stopped asking for his daddy, as his mummy had wanted him to; the little boy had stopped speaking any words at all!

She squeezed Caleb's hand where it still held hers. 'You've reached him now, Caleb; that's the important thing.' She tried to reassure him. 'It will take a little time for him to relax totally with people again, but he's made the first step, he's talking again. Just give him time,' she encouraged as he still looked uncertain. 'Adam loves you, Caleb,' she said with certainty. 'The main thing is, you've managed to reassure him he wasn't responsible for his mother's death; everything else will fall into place. With time,' she added again pointedly. It was only natural that Adam would continue to be a little reticent, but she was sure he would one day be the happy and relaxed Adam his father remembered.

Caleb shook his head. 'Until you put that theory to me, I was completely unaware—!' He sighed self-disgustedly. 'I might never have realised—'

'Of course you would,' Cat cut in briskly. 'You just had your own feelings concerning your wife's death to deal with—'

'I didn't love her any more, Cat,' he rasped. 'I hadn't loved her for a very long time.'

She swallowed hard. 'The loss of any life is difficult to bear, Caleb, but Alicia was the mother of your son. It will just keep getting better from now on, you'll see,' she asserted. Secure in his father's love and approval, Adam could only flourish, she was sure.

She wouldn't mind flourishing a little like that herself!

His other hand moved to touch the curls at her temple. 'Such a wise head on such young shoulders—'

'I'm not that young, Caleb,' she rejoined scathingly, all the time her heart beating faster at his closeness.

'Sometimes I think—'

'One prawn salad, and one steak pie—without chips,' Hayley announced efficiently, placing their meals on the table in front of them.

There was complete silence at their table for at least thirty seconds after Hayley had gone back behind the bar, Cat and Caleb just looking at each other. And then they both began to laugh. Their conversation had been so intense—too intense!—only to be interrupted with 'One prawn salad, and one steak pie—without chips'! That intensity had been reduced to the banal!

But it was an intensity that had needed breaking, Cat decided as they both began to eat, any conversation between them flowing smoothly and naturally now rather than guardedly as it had been before.

In fact, they were so relaxed in each other's company when they left the pub a couple of hours later that Caleb handed her his car keys to drive them the short distance back to the village! It wasn't because he had had too much wine to drink either, both of them sticking to that one glass of wine, before moving on to coffee and then mineral water.

'Nice car,' Cat told him as she turned the BMW round in the car park before heading for home.

'Good driver,' Caleb murmured after a couple of minutes, head back against the seat, his eyes closed. 'But then, I knew you would be.'

'And just how could you possibly know that?' Cat demanded.

He glanced across at her with warm grey eyes. 'You don't give half measures, Cat—in anything!'

She turned her attention quickly back to the road ahead, a shadow in her eyes as she knew she could never tell this man how totally in love with him she was. Because this evening spent with him, in relaxed conversation once they had talked about Adam, had only deepened that emotion. What she was going to do about it she had no idea. And at this particular moment, enjoying his company as she was, she didn't care!

Nor did she care a few minutes later when, having parked the car in the drive of Rose Cottage, Caleb turned and drew her into his arms, his mouth coming down gently on hers, that gentleness quickly disappearing—for both of them—as passion took over.

Caleb's hands moved restlessly across her back, one of those hands moving to cup the pertness of her breast, Cat groaning low in her throat at the frission of physical pleasure that instantly warmed her body.

It was always like this between them, and even as she responded to Caleb's caresses Cat knew that it just wasn't enough. She wanted more. So much more, moving restlessly in her seat behind the wheel of the car— Good grief, she was sitting in a car, her arms wrapped shamelessly about Caleb, their kisses heated to say the least!

As if she had somehow communicated the ridiculousness of their situation to Caleb, he began to chuckle, moving slightly so that his forehead rested on hers, both of them softly laughing now. 'It's been more years than I care to remember…!' He chuckled wryly.

'Than I want to know!' she acknowledged. 'You do realise Lilley probably has a pair of binoculars trained on us at this very minute?'

Caleb looked at her with laughing eyes. 'Do you care?' The hand that rested at her nape lightly played with the silky red curls there.

'No,' Cat answered honestly. 'Since you arrived my reputation has been shot with her, anyway. But even so—' she grimaced ruefully '—I think we should put a stop to this and go inside and check on Kitty and Adam.'

'You're right.' He straightened reluctantly. 'I've enjoyed tonight, Cat,' he paused to tell her huskily. 'It's the first time I've been able to completely relax since—since the evening we spent together last time,' he realised.

'I'm glad,' Cat murmured then got out of the car and followed him into the cottage.

Kitty looked up at them both happily as they entered the

sitting-room, putting away the book she had been reading. 'Adam has been asleep for hours,' she assured Caleb as she stood up. 'He's no trouble at all. So any time you need a babysitter in future just give me a call,' she offered.

'I might keep you to that, Kitty,' Caleb warned, with a warm glance at a red-faced Cat.

Kitty also glanced at Cat. 'As I said, any time.'

But it was an assurance that made Cat feel slightly uneasy, as it seemed to suggest that she and Caleb were a couple. And while that wasn't something she was averse to—how could she be when minutes ago she had wanted nothing less than for Caleb to make love to her?—she wasn't altogether sure Caleb would like the implication. After all, they had only spent two evenings together—she didn't count the evening when she had come here to talk to him about Adam—which hardly amounted to a relationship, let alone anything else.

Except that she knew she was in love with him...

'Time we were going, I think, Kitty.' Her voice sounded sharper in her embarrassment than she had intended, but there was little she could do to change that once she had spoken, Caleb looking across at her with narrowed eyes.

'Of course,' Kitty accepted gracefully. 'I'll just—'

'Goodnight, then, Caleb.' Cat interrupted what she was sure was going to be Kitty's diplomatic disappearance out to the car while Cat and Caleb said goodnight properly. She did not want to make any long-drawn-out goodnights to Caleb!

'Goodbye, Cat,' he drawled, easily able, it seemed, to read the reason for her hasty departure.

But not all of it, Cat sincerely hoped as she and Kitty drove home together in Kitty's car. Because Cat had realised, after entering Rose Cottage, that although he had had plenty of opportunity this evening Caleb still hadn't men-

tioned that he knew who Kitty really was. When he would
have been perfectly within his rights to have said something; it wasn't everyone that had the famous Katherine
Maitland babysitting their son!

'Did you have a good evening?'

'Very good, thank you,' Cat answered Kitty, behind the
wheel once again; she had driven two vehicles this evening,
and neither of them was her own!

'I knew Caleb was a nice man,' Kitty said with satisfaction. 'As I told you, there's never been anything wrong with
my taste in men!'

Maybe not, but she doubted Kitty could be quite so sure
concerning her opinion of Toby when they arrived home a
few minutes later to find Kate sitting at the kitchen table
crying as if her heart were about to break!

CHAPTER THIRTEEN

'WHAT is it?' Cat gasped her shock even as she moved forward to put comforting arms around Kate. 'What on earth's happened?' she persisted worriedly; whatever it was she wasn't about to let Toby get away with it!

'Something awful for Kate to be this upset.' Kitty stood concernedly at Kate's other side.

'I'm not upset!' Kate looked up to tell them vehemently, blue eyes seeming to flash fire. 'Upset is far too mild a word to describe how I feel; I'm furious! So much so that if I hadn't left Toby's when I did I think I would actually have hit him!'

Toby hadn't— He couldn't have—

'He's a lousy, rotten, sneaky, two-faced traitor!' Kate spat the words out angrily, two deep spots of colour in her cheeks now.

No, it didn't sound as if Toby had tried to make love to Kate, after all. But he had certainly done something!

'I'll put the kettle on and make us all a nice cup of tea,' Kitty said firmly. 'Then—if you would like to—perhaps you could explain to us what Toby has done, Kate?' she urged, suiting her actions to her words as she made the tea.

'Make that tea for four,' Toby said as he entered the kitchen through the side door.

'Get out!' Kate told him furiously as she stood up. 'I told you—'

'This doesn't only concern you, Kate,' Toby interrupted grimly, looking completely unlike his usual boyish self, lines etched beside his eyes and mouth, making him look every one of his thirty-five years. 'I didn't have to tell you,

166

Kate,' he went on as she continued to glare at him. 'I could have just left here, gone ahead with the exhibition as planned, with none of you any the wiser—'

'Until the exhibition,' Kate cut in stubbornly. 'Then I think we might have been a little more than *wise* to you— don't you?' she scorned.

He sighed, shaking his head. 'You didn't give me a chance to explain earlier—'

'Because there's nothing to explain,' Kate admonished him heatedly. 'The existence of the painting is self-explanatory!'

'What you didn't give me a chance to tell you earlier was that it's been withdrawn from the exhibition, Kate,' he told her quietly.

Kate became suddenly still, looking at him suspiciously. 'I don't believe you,' she said finally.

Toby drew in a ragged breath before turning to look at Cat and Kitty, the two of them standing as still as statues as the scene unfolded before them. One thing was more than obvious in this emotional exchange: Kate and Toby were in love with each other!

They were so different, Cat knew, Kate usually calm and controlled, Toby the teasing, frivolous one, and yet at this moment it was Toby who was calm and controlled, Kate so angry and out of control that Cat barely recognised her.

'I have a present for you, Kitty,' Toby said. 'I have it outside in my car.'

Kitty looked puzzled. 'A present for me...?'

He nodded abruptly. 'You'll understand when you see it,' he assured her before turning and going back outside.

Cat looked across at Kate, wanting to ask her what was going on, but Kate was white with tension now, and she looked as if she was holding onto any self-control she still had by a very thin thread. Cat's own pleasantly relaxed evening with Caleb seemed as if it had happened days ago instead of minutes!

When the telephone began to ring out in the hallway at that moment, Cat somehow knew that it was going to be Caleb. It was as if thinking about him had somehow communicated her distress to him, prompting him to ring her. Which was silly; he was probably just telephoning to check that she and Kitty had got home safely!

'I'll go,' she told Kate and Kitty before either of them had a chance to move, hurrying to answer the call.

'Cat?' Caleb greeted huskily as soon as she placed the receiver to her ear.

'Yes?' she replied almost in a whisper; after all, they appeared to be in the middle of a family crisis!

'I just wanted to say goodnight to you. And to tell you I had a wonderful evening,' he said gruffly.

So much for communicating her distress to him! 'So did I,' she assured him warmly, still keeping her voice low.

'Cat, we have to talk,' Caleb told her.

She tensed. 'What about?' After all, they had spent most of the evening talking!

'Oh, Cat, you have to realise that I— Why are you whispering?' He suddenly seemed to realise that was exactly what she was doing.

But Cat wanted to know what it was she must realise! She realised that he what? Liked her? Desired her? *What?*

'Cat?' he prompted sharply.

She sighed, knowing that he wasn't going to satisfy her curiosity, that he had moved on from that half-finished comment. 'It's late, Caleb,' she excused, keeping her voice low as if to emphasise the point; goodness knew what he would make of it if he should know of the scene unfolding in the kitchen right this minute! There was still so much that Caleb didn't know... 'I don't want to disturb the others—' Even as she made the claim the sound of raised voices—Kate and Toby's—could be heard coming from the kitchen.

'It sounds as if they are already disturbed,' Caleb commented drily, obviously also having heard the raised voices. 'Surely that isn't Kate and Kitty?' He sounded doubtful.

'Er—no,' Cat confirmed reluctantly. 'Toby called in, and—'

'Westward is there?' Caleb put in harshly.

Cat gave an inward groan; to each other, these two men were like red rags to bulls! 'I told you, he called in—'

'At eleven o'clock at night?' Caleb interrupted scornfully. 'And I thought he and Kate were spending the evening together?' he pressed on suspiciously.

'They did. I— It's a bit complicated, Caleb.' But at least she could no longer hear raised voices coming from the kitchen!

'How complicated?' he returned bluntly.

Remembering Kate's earlier vehemence... 'Very,' Cat said wearily. 'Thank you for calling, Caleb, but I—I really do have to go now.' The silence from the kitchen now was almost as unnerving as the shouting had been! 'I'll see you in the morning.'

'You—'

'I really do have to go, Caleb.' She rang off before he could finish what he was saying, hurrying back to the kitchen now. She could talk to Caleb tomorrow, when she knew exactly what was going on. Because at the moment she really had no idea!

But she knew exactly what was going on as soon as she entered the kitchen and saw the painting...!

It was impossible to miss as it stood on the kitchen table, propped back against the wall; it was at least five feet wide, and four feet high.

Cat stared at it, blinking rapidly, rendered as speechless as Kate and Kitty appeared to be.

'It's called *Time*,' Toby supplied when it appeared she couldn't look away from the painting.

The reason for the title was obvious, the painting a study in three distinct periods of a woman's life, the young woman on the verge of life and love, the middle-aged woman, disillusioned by what that life and love had shown her, and finally the elderly woman, still beautiful, having attained an inner serenity that showed in every masterly brush-stroke.

That woman was Kitty!

As a work of art, it was undoubtedly a masterpiece; as a study of the woman Cat knew and loved, it was so beautifully crafted that it made her want to cry. But Kitty wasn't just someone that she knew and loved.

The woman in the painting, in all three guises, wasn't Kitty at all—she was Katherine Maitland...!

She turned accusing green eyes on Toby. 'You knew,' she breathed softly, disbelievingly. 'All this time, you knew...!' And she had dismissed Toby—several times—as harmless!

He drew in a sharp breath. 'I knew before I even met any of you,' he confirmed grimly, looking apologetically at the still silent Kitty. 'My agent—the mysterious blonde I was once seen with, incidentally, Cat,' he told her drily, 'she decided that I needed a focus for my next exhibition, something that would bring my work to the attention of a wider audience. After several false starts,' he went on, 'I tracked down Katherine Maitland, England's answer to Greta Garbo, as having lived in this house before her disappearance from public life. I could hardly believe my luck when the house now appeared to be owned by the granddaughters of Katherine Maitland! It was just too much of a coincidence, I'm afraid. And from there it wasn't too difficult to work out that Kitty was actually the person I was really looking for!' He shook his head ruefully.

'Reynolds once asked me why I chose this particular locality to rent a cottage, Cat,' he said. 'So now you know!'

So now she knew... And she wished she didn't. She had liked Toby, trusted him, and he had done this!

'This really is an amazing painting, Toby.' Kitty was the one to answer him huskily. 'How on earth did you manage to capture me looking quite so—?'

'Serene?' Toby put in with enthusiasm. 'Because that's what you are, Kitty,' he told her warmly. 'I've come to admire you so much these last few months—'

'Oh, spare us all that!' Kate put in scathingly. 'You used us, Toby. All of us. As you've already admitted, you've always known exactly who we all are. You came to the village, used our friendship, just so that you could paint *that*!' She glared across at the painting.

Cat could understand her vehemence, felt betrayed herself—and she wasn't in love with Toby, as she was now sure Kate was. But at the same time, like Kitty, she could see the beauty of the painting, the thirst for life in the young Katherine, then the disillusionment she had ultimately known in that life, and finally that serenity.

It was a truly beautiful painting, one that Toby could be suitably proud of—

For the second time in the last fifteen minutes the kitchen door opened and someone walked in unannounced—and this time it was Caleb!

Cat stared at him, noting the solemnness of his expression, his piercing eyes as he looked at Toby.

What had he done with Adam? Surely he hadn't just left him? If Adam should wake up—

'I grabbed a passing neighbour and asked her to sit with him,' Caleb told her as he easily read her thoughts. 'Actually, that isn't so far from the truth. Lilley was out walking her dog, and— Good God!' He came to a sudden halt as he saw the painting for the first time.

While he stared at it, Cat's mind reeled. Lilley! He had asked Lilley to sit with Adam while he came here? She didn't even want to think about what that woman would be saying about his extraordinary behaviour tomorrow at the post office!

Caleb blinked, turning to Toby. 'Extraordinary,' he murmured softly. 'Is it for sale?'

'Caleb!' Cat gasped her outrage.

'Not for me,' he assured her gently. 'I would buy it for *you*.'

'Me?' She stiffened warily. 'But why? I don't—'

'A painting of this calibre should stay in the family,' Caleb said firmly. 'And, as Kitty's granddaughter, you are certainly that!'

Cat stared at him. First Toby and now...! Did everyone know?

It had been a major decision for Kitty to leave Ireland, where she had lived for several years in relative obscurity, so that she might once again live in her beloved England. They had been so careful when buying this house, making sure the name Maitland never came into it, and as an extra precaution Kate and Cat had decided it might be better if Caitlin Rourke, the more well-known granddaughter of Katherine Maitland, didn't feature too prominently either. As Kate's grandmother, Kitty's anonimity could be retained.

But she was Cat's grandmother too, and Kate was her cousin, the cousin who had come to live with Cat's family when she was a baby, the baby cousin Cat had been so jealous of all those years ago...

And Caleb knew all that. How long had he known?

'I gave Caleb a guided tour of the house this afternoon, Cat.' Kitty was the one to tell her. 'And afterwards Caleb and I had quite a chat.' She smiled across at him warmly.

Now she knew why he hadn't referred back to knowing

Kitty was Katherine Maitland earlier this evening—he'd had no need to, having already spoken to Kitty herself!

'I wasn't going behind your back,' he defended as Cat looked at him accusingly. 'Kitty mentioned the subject to me first,' he insisted as Cat still looked sceptical.

'It's true, Cat,' her grandmother told her. 'It's become more and more obvious to me, this last week in particular, that my presence here, this protective responsibility you and Kate both feel towards me, is affecting your lives—'

'That isn't true.' Kate was the first to protest.

But Cat wasn't far behind her. 'It certainly isn't!' she said forcefully.

Along with baby Kate, their grandmother had come to live with them in Ireland too, the two girls going to school together, eventually going off to college together seven years ago too. So Cat could never remember a time when they weren't all together, and it had seemed the most natural thing in the world, when Kitty had expressed a wish to live in England again, that her two granddaughters would live with her. They both loved Kitty, would stop anything, and anyone, from ever hurting her. As she had once been hurt so badly...

'It is affecting you and Kate both forming natural attachments,' Kitty continued determinedly. 'Good grief, the two of you are twenty-five now; it's time one, or both, of you made me a great-grandmother! And if I'm not mistaken,' she added happily, 'we have the two men here who will willingly be your partners in doing that!'

'Grandmother!'

'Kitty!'

Both Cat and Kate groaned their embarrassment, neither of them able to look at either of those two men.

'My contribution will be with Cat, I hope,' Caleb drawled with amusement. 'One of your granddaughters is quite enough for any man to handle, Kitty.'

'Wait until you're asked,' Cat snapped, eyes flashing deeply green, her embarrassment still acute.

'Forget the equality thing this time, Cat,' he told her. 'When it comes to a proposal—I'll be the one to do the asking!'

'You—'

'Will you marry me, Caitlin Rourke?' he continued, the mildness of his tone belied by the anxiety in his eyes.

'I—'

'I'm going back to Ireland to live with your mother and father, Cat,' Kitty put in softly, at the same time making Cat very aware that she wasn't to figure in any answer she might care to give Caleb. 'I've done what I needed to do, my dears. Lived in this house again, laid my ghosts to rest; but now I think it's time I went back home to Ireland. Yes, I did say home.' She smiled at Cat and Kate as they looked at her in surprise. 'Until I actually came back here I hadn't realised just how much I have come to love Ireland, to think of that as my home.'

Cat was still reeling from the shock of Caleb's proposal. Was he serious?

'I'm sure you are both aware of the history behind my early retirement from public life.' Kitty turned to the two men present. 'It was a wonderful career, but it ultimately caused my family so much unhappiness,' she sighed, giving a sad shake of her head. 'My two daughters grew up in a blaze of publicity that seemed to follow them wherever they went. They weren't allowed to make the mistakes of other teenagers. At least, not without it appearing in some damned newspaper,' she added bitterly. 'My eldest daughter, Amanda, escaped from it when she met and married Michael. Michael protects what is his, and that includes his wife and daughter.' She smiled affectionately at Cat.

Cat gave her a tearful smile back, knowing how much

talking about all of this still hurt her grandmother. How it had hurt all of the family at the time...

Kitty drew in a deep breath. 'My youngest daughter wasn't so lucky. She was ten years younger than Amanda, and after her father died she became the focus of my world. Unfortunately, she became the focus of the media world too!' She sighed her anger at the constant hounding her youngest daughter had been subjected to. 'Was it any wonder then that Patty fell in love with a completely unsuitable man? I'm sorry, Kate.' She smiled gently at her younger granddaughter. 'He was your father, I know, but—'

'It's all right, Kitty,' Kate assured her huskily. 'I don't have any illusions where he's concerned!'

'I do so wish— Wishing won't change what happened,' Kitty continued determinedly. 'Patty fell in love with Sean Brady,' she told Caleb and Toby. 'And although I could see him for what he was—a fortune-hunter—Patty wouldn't have a word said against him. She married him,' she said heavily. 'Against my wishes. But once she was his wife there was nothing that could be done, except grin and bear it. But when Patty became pregnant he began to be violent towards her.'

She shook her head. 'It wasn't a happy marriage, and when Patty was in hospital giving birth Sean was finally located in bed with another woman! Patty remained strong until she came out of hospital, but the reporters, sensing they were on to a Maitland family scandal, hounded the poor girl day and night.'

Kitty swallowed hard. 'When Kate was only two months old, with Sean out spending the night with yet another woman, Patty swallowed a bottle of pills.' She blinked back the tears the memory of the death of her youngest child could still produce. 'Is it any wonder I shied away from public life after that? That I gave up my career, packed up my granddaughter and—?'

'And moved to Ireland to live with Amanda and her husband Michael,' Caleb finished for her throatily. 'I was a fan, Cat,' he reminded her as she frowned across at him. 'I knew that Katherine's eldest daughter had married the jockey Michael Rourke, that you had to be their daughter. But I never had any intention of abusing that knowledge.' His voice hardened as he turned to look at Toby with glacial eyes.

Toby grimly returned his stare. 'Before you arrived I had made Kitty a present of the painting!'

'Big of you,' Caleb scorned. 'Conscience get the better of you?'

'No,' Toby ground out. 'Like you, I fell in love.'

Caleb's hands became clenched at his sides. 'You had your chance with Cat, Westward,' he bit out harshly, 'and you blew it! Now get out, and—'

'I fell in love with Kate, Reynolds,' Toby corrected him scathingly, turning to look beseechingly at a now stunned Kate. 'I admit I tried to use you all,' he said gruffly. 'When it all began it was just a painting to me. But as I got to know you all,' he continued as Kate would have spoken, 'it became more and more obvious to me that I couldn't expose Kitty to the sort of publicity my painting was sure to bring down on her, on all of you—'

'Modesty isn't something you know too much about, is it?' Caleb taunted.

Toby looked at him. 'I doubt it's something you're too familiar with, either!'

'We weren't discussing me,' Caleb drawled insultingly. 'I'm not the one who wormed his way in here under false pretences—'

'Now listen here—'

'Gentlemen, gentlemen.' Kitty silenced them both as she stood up, smiling cajolingly. 'I suggest, as the two of you are probably going to be related through marriage very shortly, that you stop exchanging insults and concentrate on my granddaughters instead! As for the painting, Toby,' she said, 'it really is a masterpiece, and I'm sure it would be as successful as you suggested it would. I just—'

'It's yours, Kitty,' Toby assured her firmly.

She reached out to gently touch him on the cheek. 'Thank you. Now I'm off to bed,' she announced briskly. 'I'm not as young as I was, and I think we're all going to have a busy time ahead of us. My move back to Ireland. Two weddings to arrange—'

'I think I have to do the asking first, Kitty,' Toby told her drily. 'Let alone be accepted!'

'Well, get on with it, then,' she advised, kissing Cat and Kate goodnight on the cheek. 'I like them both very much,' was her parting comment.

In other words, Cat knew, and she was sure that Kate did too, Kitty approved of these two men in their lives! But Kate looked as embarrassed by the situation their grandmother had left them in as Cat felt!

'Shall we go through to the sitting-room and give Kate and Toby some privacy?' Caleb prompted her as he opened the door for them to leave the room.

Cat glanced across at Kate. Her cousin had barely spoken for the last few minutes, and not at all since Toby had announced he had fallen in love with her.

The two of them had been babies together, grown up together, were closer than most sisters, and as she looked at Kate she knew that Toby's explanation still hadn't overcome Kate's feelings of having been betrayed...

Cat moved to her side, putting a gentle hand on her arm. 'Kitty loves the painting. And there's been no real harm done—'

'But—'

'Give the man a chance, Kate.' Caleb spoke up huskily.

'We all make mistakes. At least Toby has been able to do something about his.'

Was Caleb trying to rectify his own? Cat wondered as the two of them went to the sitting-room together. With her? Did he believe that marriage to her would be more successful than it had been with Alicia?

If he really meant his proposal. Which Cat still wasn't a hundred per cent sure of. And if he was serious could she accept? Could she overcome this mistrust she had of men by becoming Caleb's wife? Oh, how she wanted to!

Caleb was nothing like Graham, had tried to protect Kitty as much as she had, had even wanted to buy Toby's painting for her so that they could continue that protection. If only Caleb had meant that marriage proposal...

'Cat,' he murmured softly, his gaze gentle as she looked at him almost shyly. 'I realise we haven't known each other very long, but—I love you,' he told her forcefully. 'The four days that Adam and I were away I was unable to think of anything else. I've never loved anyone the way I love you. You're loyal, truthful, caring, loving, beautiful—everything I could ever want. I even love the way you answer me back! In fact—' he drew in a ragged breath '—I wish you would say something now! If I'm just standing here making an idiot of myself, then for God's sake stop me now!' He looked at her with pained eyes.

Caleb, usually arrogant, self-assured, was neither of those things at this moment. Because he loved her—and he didn't know if she loved him in return!

She crossed the room quickly, her arms going about his waist as she rested her head against his chest. 'You aren't making a fool of yourself! I love you,' she told him strongly, knowing the time had come for putting the past behind her. 'You asked me once about the man who had—who had hurt me, remember? And I dismissed the suggestion.' She sighed. 'You were right, Caleb. There was someone. He used me to get to Kitty.' She paused. 'I was on the point of marrying him when I realised my mistake.' She shuddered at the memory of her humiliation that night in Graham's apartment. 'It's made me—'

'The bastard!' Caleb ground out fiercely. 'Who—?'

'He isn't important any more, Caleb,' she soothed—realising for the first time that it was true. Caleb wasn't Graham, was nothing like him, was as different as the sun was from the moon. Caleb wanted to love and look after her, Graham had only wanted to use her. 'I love you, Caleb,' she told him without reserve. 'And I so much want to be with you. And Adam.'

'Always?'

'Always,' she nodded.

'As my wife?'

'Oh, yes, please,' she accepted warmly, at last feeling his arms come about her and hold her tightly against him. As if he never wanted to let her go. She looked up at him with eyes that shone with her love for him. 'I would love to be your wife, Caleb.'

'Thank you,' he said, very much as Kitty had to Toby minutes ago with regard to the gift of the painting. Caleb's head lowered as his lips claimed hers, passion quickly flaring out of control. As it always did between them. As it always would.

It was some time later, with Cat comfortably nestled in Caleb's arms as they sat together on the sofa, that she suddenly remembered Caleb had left Lilley at the cottage looking after Adam.

He chuckled when she reminded him, fingers playing with her red curls, something he seemed to enjoy doing almost as much as kissing her. 'I'll invite her to the wedding when I get back,' Caleb murmured huskily. 'She'll love that. Especially,' he added ruefully, 'when I tell her it's going to be a double wedding! Because I'm sure it's going to be; those two love each other; they'll work things out.'

And it was only fitting, Cat acknowledged as she shared his laughter, that she and Kate should share their wedding day; they had shared so much already...

EPILOGUE

'EVERYTHING okay with you today?' Caleb kissed Cat lightly on the lips before bending to kiss the downy softness of their daughter's cheek as she nestled against Cat's breast, taking the last of her feed.

Everything was perfect. Much more so than she could ever have imagined. She and Caleb had been married just over a year now, and it had been a year filled with happiness.

She and Kate still ran their playschool, both Caleb and Toby in agreement when told of their wives' wish to carry on working after their marriages. And Clive House, once divided up into Kitty's part of the house, and that of Cat and Kate, now housed both married couples, living in perfect harmony on their own sides. Adam was in his element surrounded by this loving family, a constant visitor to his aunty Kate and uncle Toby, and with his cat for a pet— having opted for Maddie's black kitten with the white paws—Adam's life was as perfect as Cat considered her own to be.

They had been a little worried how Adam would view having a baby brother or sister, but when Annabelle had been born six weeks ago it was Adam who'd run excitedly to tell his aunty and uncle about her.

Although Adam's joy and pleasure in his baby half-sister could in no way match that of his father in his daughter…!

Caleb had taken a part-time position at the university in York, spending the rest of his time writing and being with his family. He had been at Cat's side on the night their daughter was born, unashamed tears falling down his cheeks when the tiny little girl, with her mother's red hair, was placed lovingly into his arms.

It had been a wonderful year, a marvellous year, for them all, and Cat knew that their love for each other had only deepened and grown.

'It's been a lovely day,' she assured Caleb smilingly now, standing up to place their daughter in her crib and settle her down for the night.

'You've seemed a little—preoccupied this evening.' Caleb looked across at her as he prepared himself for bed.

How well he knew her, this husband of hers. In the past year he had often seemed to know what would make her happy before she had realised it herself. Their wedding, jointly with Kate and Toby, had taken place in Ireland, and had been attended by their relatives and friends there. The decision for them all to live at Clive House, suitably divided so as to give all of them their own privacy, but at the same time meaning that she and Kate—a Kate who was now six months pregnant herself—could still be family, had been amicably made by Caleb and Toby. In fact, the two men had become the best of friends, Toby now seeking the other man's advice about having a pregnant wife. Caleb had just advised him to give Kate the chocolate biscuits and pickled eggs, and not to worry about it!

Yes, it had been a good year, a happy year; it was impossible now for Cat to imagine life without Caleb at her side, and Adam as her son.

She got into bed next to Caleb, having already bathed before feeding the baby. 'Annabelle had her six-week check-up today,' she told her husband.

He instantly looked concerned. 'Is she—?'

'She's wonderful, Caleb,' Cat assured him laughingly. 'Absolutely perfect in every way.'

'Then—'

'I had my check-up too,' she told him.

It had been so long since she and Caleb had made love, she almost felt as shy as she had on their wedding night. Although that had been a shyness Caleb had quickly dispensed with, that first night of love as joyful as all the nights since had been. Even her pregnancy hadn't lessened their desire for each other; in fact, it had been rather fun!

But Annabelle's birth had brought an abrupt end to their lovemaking. Briefly, Cat hoped. Although she now felt a little hesitant about telling Caleb she was more than ready for them to resume making love! So ready she ached with wanting him!

'Any problems?' He looked anxious.

'None at all,' she assured him warmly; how did one go about asking one's husband to make love to one?

'But that's good, isn't it?' Caleb looked puzzled now.

'Caleb.' She reached up and put her arms about his neck. 'You aren't making this at all easy for me!'

He shook his head. 'That's probably because I don't know what the problem is!' he said exasperatedly.

She gave a laugh. 'That's my whole point—there isn't one! The doctor has given me the go-ahead, Caleb,' she told him expectantly.

For several more seconds he looked blank, and then his expression slowly changed as her meaning became clear to him. But instead of the pleasure she had expected to see in his face she saw apprehension...!

She drew back slightly. 'What is it, Caleb? Don't you— don't you want me any more?' She was already back to the weight she had been before her pregnancy, but she was aware that she had changed shape slightly, her breasts fuller, her thighs more slender; perhaps Caleb no longer found her attractive...?

'Don't be so damned stupid!' His harsh response dispensed with that thought. 'I wanted you from the moment I first saw you. But you're even more desirable to me now than you were before—softer, so utterly feminine. I want you every time I look at you, Cat,' he assured her deeply.

'Then—'

'Do *you* want me, Cat?' He frowned his uncertainty. '*Really* want me? Or are you just—are you just—'

Oh, Caleb, her darling Caleb; all this time, all these weeks of gentleness and caring, he had believed she would never want to make love to him again. As Alicia hadn't...

Her arms tightened about his neck. 'I haven't been pre-occupied this evening, my darling, I've been wishing the evening away, longing for the time we could come to bed, Adam and Annabelle safely tucked up in their beds, and make long glorious love together!'

Caleb's tension left him, the past wiped away in the face of her honesty. 'Oh, Cat,' he groaned. 'My darling, desirable Cat!' He bent to kiss her. 'I love you so much,' he murmured huskily, both of them trembling in anticipation of the pleasure they were about to share. 'I'll always love you,' he promised as his lips claimed hers.

And Cat knew she would always love and want him too.

Perfection.

If you enjoyed what you just read,
then we've got an offer you can't resist!

Take 2 bestselling love stories FREE!

Plus get a FREE surprise gift!

Clip this page and mail it to Harlequin Reader Service®

IN U.S.A.	IN CANADA
3010 Walden Ave.	P.O. Box 609
P.O. Box 1867	Fort Erie, Ontario
Buffalo, N.Y. 14240-1867	L2A 5X3

YES! Please send me 2 free Harlequin Presents® novels and my free surprise gift. Then send me 6 brand-new novels every month, which I will receive months before they're available in stores. In the U.S.A., bill me at the bargain price of $3.12 plus 25¢ delivery per book and applicable sales tax, if any*. In Canada, bill me at the bargain price of $3.49 plus 25¢ delivery per book and applicable taxes**. That's the complete price and a savings of over 10% off the cover prices—what a great deal! I understand that accepting the 2 free books and gift places me under no obligation ever to buy any books. I can always return a shipment and cancel at any time. Even if I never buy another book from Harlequin, the 2 free books and gift are mine to keep forever. So why not take us up on our invitation. You'll be glad you did!

106 HEN CNER

306 HEN CNES

Name _____ (PLEASE PRINT) _____

Address _____ Apt.# _____

City _____ State/Prov. _____ Zip/Postal Code _____

* Terms and prices subject to change without notice. Sales tax applicable in N.Y.

** Canadian residents will be charged applicable provincial taxes and GST.
  All orders subject to approval. Offer limited to one per household.
  ® are registered trademarks of Harlequin Enterprises Limited.

PRES99   ©1998 Harlequin Enterprises Limited

Return to the charm of the Regency era with

GEORGETTE HEYER,

creator of the modern Regency genre.

Enjoy six romantic collector's editions with forewords
by some of today's bestselling romance authors,

**Nora Roberts, Mary Jo Putney,
Jo Beverley, Mary Balogh,
Theresa Medeiros and Kasey Michaels.**

Frederica
On sale February 2000
The Nonesuch
On sale March 2000
The Convenient Marriage
On sale April 2000
Cousin Kate
On sale May 2000
The Talisman Ring
On sale June 2000
The Corinthian
On sale July 2000

Available at your favorite retail outlet.

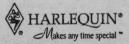

HARLEQUIN®
Makes any time special ™

Visit us at www.romance.net

PHGHGEN

Come escape with Harlequin's new

Series Sampler

Four great full-length Harlequin novels bound together in one fabulous volume and at an unbelievable price.

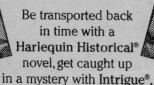

Be transported back in time with a Harlequin Historical® novel, get caught up in a mystery with Intrigue®, be tempted by a hot, sizzling romance with Harlequin Temptation®, or just enjoy a down-home all-American read with American Romance®.

You won't be able to put this collection down!

On sale February 2000 at your favorite retail outlet.

HARLEQUIN®
Makes any time special ™

Visit us at www.romance.net

PHESC

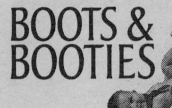

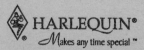